HELLBOUND

D1290630

COURTNEY SIGLER

PAGE PUBLISHING, INC.
New York, NY

First originally published by Page Publishing, Inc. 2018

ISBN 978-1-64082-531-4 (Paperback)
ISBN 978-1-64082-532-1 (Digital)

Printed in the United States of America

For Mark, Austin, Randal, and Caleb—
who are and will always be my cherished.

TROUBLING CALL

"Hi, Mrs. Jacobs. This is Dr. Dobbler. I've just gotten off the phone with Dr. Ayen, Thomas's neurologist, and she says the tests are unchanged. This is a good thing, Jenna. She said the noise he's been making is most likely made by muscle contractions in his diaphragm and voice box. She said it's harmless and nothing to worry about. I beg you to let this pursuit go. Thomas needs you. I just don't want him to be dragged around the country again so you can search for answers that aren't there."

Click. Jenna's expression froze with Dr. Dobbler's empty words. She felt the pit deep within her grow; it ached to her that something was wrong. She was alone in her thinking—deemed mad and paranoid by most the medical staff, maybe even her own husband. Frustration led her to the verge of tears until she turned to her son, her world. Her somber face faded to childlike smile. Her worries left her briefly as Thomas smiled back at her.

Jenna Jacobs was forty-six, and she still carried the restlessness of her youth. She was born to a small town in Ohio—the same town as her husband, Alan. They had been lovers in high school. Their passion had whirlwound great ambition in Jenna, and after high school, she went to college on the East Coast. First in pursuit of a medical degree and then to Paris to study art—with each field of study a new location: business was studied in New York, a semester of architecture in Arizona. She hungered for knowledge and adventure and felt direction would only slow her down. Her passion turned to traveling, seeing the world, different cultures. She left school for the Peace Corps at the age twenty-six where she began writing Alan again. With their letters they realized that their love never faded, never died. It only waited as hot coals do for the opportunity to burn strong and wild.

Alan Jacobs was now operating a computer manufacturing shop, forty-five miles from where he grew up. He had gotten his degree at the local community college and had advanced in status as the company itself had advanced. He was steady, grounded, and strong. His one true pursuit had been Jenna. His lone adventure was a surprise trip to Africa, where he had surprised Jenna with a proposal in marriage. That was the beginning of their life together.

Jenna's next pursuit was a child. With each passing year, the longing for a child grew. They lingered on the adoption waiting list. The desperation of this now-forty-three-year-old woman had left her feeling broken. A fading hope remained. The doctor said in-vitro is becoming much more successful but stressed the increasing risk of health problems to mothers over forty years old. They tried and failed. The failure crippled Jenna spirit, but after time and Alan's coaxing, they tried again. Thomas was born to Dayton, Ohio, in the fall of 1997. Much testing confirmed that Thomas was afflicted with severe mental retardation.

Jenna and Alan were more in love now than ever. They had vowed to commit themselves to being the most supportive parents possible. Alan took overtime at work, and Jenna committed every waking moment to Thomas. She knew the latest research and worked therapies beyond the physical aspects, which included the spiritual realm of Thomas's young body. Jenna's ambition was fueled, and she and Thomas traveled to participate in the latest research at the most recognized universities. Alan's soothing spirit and drained bank account brought his family back to him.

Jenna started up working with Alan's company in the shipping and receiving department. They settled back into life. Thomas started school, and all was well—until Thomas's ninth year. Then came the sound. Only a sound at first but then defined—purposeful almost;

but purposeful speech is not realistic for a child thought to be at the mentality of a three-month-old infant. His eyes haunted her and forced soft hairs to stand on end. The continuous jerky movements remained. Could she have deceived herself again?

"But this is new," she told the doctors.

And she demanded it be addressed by only the most competent of neurologist. So it began with an end—another dead end for Jenna Jacobs.

MUNICH, GERMANY

The crowd grew restless. Teachers, doctors, psychologists all gathered in suits and skirts, cradling briefcases and notebooks, filling themselves with free muffins and coffee. A small man with thinning hair and a growing midline awkwardly marched onto the stage, raising his hands to the crowds to signal silence. He settled behind the podium.

"Ladies and gentlemen, I thank you for your presence here today. I am overwhelmed by all the excitement our research has spawn. Now I am very proud to introduce to you the engineer of all this groundbreaking therapy, Dr. William Herrington."

A much taller man poked his head beyond the partisan and gave a relaxed wave to the audience as a warm smile took over his face. He grabbed the microphone from the podium and paced the stage as he talked, continuously scanning the crowd for looks of understanding and interest.

"I have dedicated all my life to the emotional health of children. I've never had much interest in research from a personal perspective—until, that is, I met a child I could not help. His name was Dawson, and he was six years old. He landed in my office after exhausting the capacities of three other therapists. This child quite suddenly began wild tantrums, unprovoked crying spells, and extended periods where he wouldn't talk to or even look at people. This bizarre behavior was unrelieved by conventional therapy. So I began to get creative. I brainstormed with his parents, doctors, and other psychologists. Then I began mirroring his behavior. By the end of the day, I was exhausted and growing skeptical to whether this child could be helped. Slowly, he began to come around, seemingly amused by his control over my behaviors. I believe mirroring might not only have helped him feel acknowledged but opened my eyes and gave me clues to his distress. Many sessions revealed that he was having horrible dreams. They would even torment him throughout the day. You see, his mom was a believer in the purposefulness and realism of every dream. She read many books on the matter and often went to seminars. Through the years, she expressed this to her young son. He was scared to tell anyone about these horrible dreams, fearing it would get back to his mom and she would hate him—or worse, that when found out, the dreams would come to be reality. When we finally discovered what was haunting this child, we could more appropriately treat him with dream therapy and focus on the root of the problem. This may be the first story, but it is not nearly the last. Other professionals have adopted mirroring to help many other children. That's where the true research is validated, but we all know that countless hours also need to be spent in the laboratory in a more controlled setting. Now, I have for you Dr. Garland Russ, who led the experiment team. Without his commitment, none of this would be possible. Thank you."

With that, he eased down the stairs with a last sendoff wave. He blended first into the crowd and then worked through it. All eyes had found another focus, and he was able to slip into his jeep, his serenity. He let out a relieved sigh, and he melted into the seat.

Will glided through the city to his suburban home just on the outskirts. The house was brick, two stories, and had flowering vines that delicately clung to the trellis on either side of the front door. The lawn was neatly maintained as was the small flower garden that followed the entranceway sidewalk. The jeep door swung open, and his temporary peace was interrupted by a familiar noise. It was loud music that was really just muffled noise from this distance. The vibrations grew in his chest as he reached the door. He pulled open the door and braced himself against the intense noise. He awkwardly rushed about the house, trying desperately to find the source of his new stress. He raced into his bedroom and hit the power button on the stereo. He turned around inquisitively after hearing a startled moan behind him. He was momentarily paralyzed by the deep red in her hair, by the dim flickering light, and it danced on her face. She stood flawlessly and faced him. She lacked clothing and modesty. She gracefully pulled a long spring dress over her. By this time, Will's unfrozen mouth tried clumsily to speak as fury filled him.

"You need to leave." Will's voice was deep and stern. "Do you even know how old he is?"

Will scolded as she turned and silently pushed one last soft kiss on the young man's lips. Will turned quickly in disbelief and hurried out of the room. Will paced the kitchen table, cradling a beer and trying to find words. What words? His head was clouded with fury. His mind wandered back to their meeting, the intensity in his young eyes. He heard the opening and closing of the front door. The seventeen-year-old boy made his way to the kitchen. Will looked up to see a proud smile cover Hellbound's young face.

"Why my room?" Will questioned angrily.

"Have you seen my room lately? I can't bring girls there," Hellbound reasoned as Will turned away from the young man.

He was teetering on verge of anger and laughter over this situation and what had become of his life.

"That, Hellbound, was not a girl. You will wash my sheets too!" Will demanded of the youth.

Hellbound left the room to try to reconcile with his comrade by doing the simple task he had asked. If he had been Will's son, he would have taken his car for a week, or manual labor would have been sufficient punishments, but discipline was always found to be lacking. Will had taken a lot of referrals from the school counselor, even when his schedule had not permitted it, and in return Hellbound was allowed to stay in school despite fights, smoking, disobedience, protests, and numerous other offenses. Will's mind was flooded with all the phone calls and concerned conversations he had received throughout the years due to this young man. Since he was a child, he had a good heart but no concerns for social standards. He was intelligent but was hardened at an early age by the cruelties of the world.

He did not strive for acceptance and belonging as most kids did. He would do schoolwork with ease when it suited him but had refused to do any testing since he was young. He spoke like an old man who no longer had time for acceptable behavior and would say whatever harsh truth his mind had perceived. Will had to detach himself from the idea that he could turn Hellbound in an ideal, ambitious young man. Will had often teased of the youth's iritic behaviors that he was hell-bound. He'd passively blurt out "Hellbound" when he noticed the youth making compromising decisions, hoping the youth would be aware of his choices. To Will's dismay, Jackson found it to be amusing—a stamp of his alternative attitude toward the world—and so he became known to Will and close friends as Hellbound.

Will's mind wandered back on their meeting in his office. He was called after hours and begged to see this child on an emergency basis.

"He won't talk to anyone. We caught him in the allies."

Desperation overcame the social worker's voice, and she had to clear her throat to keep from cracking her voice.

Caught him? Will thought to himself.

"He looks about seven to eight, you said?" he clarified his information as it didn't seem congruent with the precautions implicated by the state social worker.

"Yes, but I don't trust his eyes. They're not the eyes of a little boy, you see. I don't know what it is, but my hair rises on end when he looks at me. Just be careful," she pleaded. "We don't know what kind of environment he came from."

Thirty minutes later, a tattered little boy was pushed into his office. His hair was shoulder-length and greasy. His clothes were much too small for him and stiffened by dried sweat and filth. He didn't have any shoes on and his feet, which were blistered and cut in a several different spots. Will was overwhelmed by the foul smell of the child. Will rose to his feet infuriated.

"Why has this child not been washed and allowed a decent outfit?" Will voiced.

The social worker defensively scolded back, "We've tried. He won't let us. He's violent to us and uses disgraceful language. I have had about all I can take with this kid, he's not fit for a foster home. He's a threat."

Will grabbed the child by the arm, and the entourage went to the doctor's office, where he had attached bathroom with shower. The doctor grabbed scissors and pulled with force on the already-stretched clothing. The child stood still as Will cut the boy's shirt and pants off. The woman had hurried to make the shower a proper temperature and readied the soap, shampoo, and a washcloth. Will noticed the deep imprints where the constricting clothing had been, along with reddened areas of excoriated skin along the armpits, waist, and groin causation of friction of the movable joints of child's thin body against the restrictive garments—Will imagined. The doctor's heart sank of the sight, but he buffered against any emotional facial expressions with a few deep breaths. He threw a blanket around the child and pushed him into the bathroom. Will looked the boy in the eyes forcefully.

"This is shampoo, it goes in your hair, then you wash it out. This is soap and a washcloth, scrub your entire body with it and rinse. Dry with this towel when you're done. Your friend here and I will be waiting in my office," Will instructed.

While the child washed, the overwhelmed woman hurried to retrieve proper clothing from the car. She pushed the clothes at Dr. Herrington, with a look that clearly told Will that she was merely an assistant now. The shower stopped, and some minutes later, a new child walked out.

"That's better," Dr. Harrington commented.

They led him to the bathroom and directed him to put on the new clothes. The child reemerged looking strong and handsome, despite his emaciation. The child truly had a look on his face that was beyond his years. There was no fear in him and no shame.

"Now," the doctor spoke assertively, "the only thing I care to discuss tonight is whether you have any people at all to look after you." Will questioned sternly.

"I don't need people to look in on me," the boy blurted arrogantly.

"Unfortunately, you're not able to decide that yet, and from the repair you came to us in, I don't agree," Will explained.

"No, I don't have any people." The child's voice matched the doctor's assertive tone.

"Where did they go?" Will inquired.

"I've never had people. I don't remember anyone anyhow," the boy rebutted.

"Where do you stay?" Will questioned.

"Anywhere, I move a lot," the boy explained.

Will was overwhelmed with questions, but he decided that it would have been too much for the child tonight.

"OK," Will signaled to the caseworker. "Just put him into foster care until we can investigate a little further into his case. He doesn't seem to be harmful now," Will concluded.

"There's no foster care he can go to. I've called for over an hour and a half in the office," the irritated social worker explained.

"Looks like you've got a new partner," Will smirked.

"I've got babies at home, Dr. Harrington—one of my own and two I'm caring for related to the foster care shortage. I'm not going to put any of them in danger," she demanded. "So, Doctor, It looks like you've got a new partner." She laughed, tightening her mouth in resistance of a laugh.

The doctor gasped at her insinuations. He argued excuses of his own, but it was obvious she had come with alternate motives, and she knew how to play hardball.

"He can stay the night, just until you find something," Will stressed.

The child called himself Jackson and had no comprehension of a last name. He spoke with a matured tongue and lacked the youthful innocence of childhood. It was soon clear to Dr. Harrington that no family short of doctorate in psychology could foster to this child. The doctor himself struggled through his bizarre mannerisms and manipulative behaviors. Will's spirit ached as the child refused to eat or drink despite reasoning. Will acted indifferent and desperately fought to keep the control of the relationship and not to be consumed by the manipulative behaviors of this broken youth. The child coyly tormented his new roommate. He roamed his new environment breaking boundaries for the simple pleasure of defying his invisible prison—amused and intrigued by the doctor's responses.

One late-night trip to the bathroom, Will heard noises from the kitchen. He peeked around the corner to find young Jackson gorging on the leftover pizza from that night's meal. The doctor crept back to bed. The next night, the doctor announced that he had had a hard day at work and they would be eating hot fudge Sundays in place of dinner. He dramatized the overwhelming taste of the sweets and let years of professional mannerisms melt away as he laughed, explaining the trials of the day and the extraordinary taste of the dessert with mouth open and fudge and whip cream sloppily running down his face and onto the chest of his suit. The doctor acted oblivious that his own messed state and called the neighbor kids over. He insisted they take the rest of the ice cream, sides, and any remotely tempting snack and beverages. He packed grocery bags and filled wagon and backpacks and insisted they enjoy the goodies because they would only go to waste. Jackson silently stood by with a numb expression. That night while the child was sorting through the empty refrigerator, debating between the leftover cooked carrots, raw rice, or dry oatmeal, he turned behind him to find one William Harrington standing in the doorway with broad shoulders and a mockingly cocky smirk. Their eyes connected just long enough to convey that the doctor had won. Then Will confidently went back to bed.

After that, Jackson stole lawn decoration and small statues from nearby neighbor only to display them in the doctor's yard. Will pretended to be pleased by the new decorations only to wait until Jackson was at school to explain the situation and pay a ridiculous amount of money for the new trinkets. Then Dr. Harrington told Jackson upon returning from school that the neighborhood association had outdone themselves this year and he must have won an honor for best landscaping. The doctor was confident he instinctually knew the difference between right and wrong and that chaos was actually what Jackson sought after. Countless other offenses earned Jackson the nickname Hellbound, who constantly was pushing beyond the invisible boundaries between right and wrong. Jackson soon adopted the name as a self-proclaimed rebel badge.

Despite frequent havoc, the doctor continued to be unwaveringly laid-back, at least on the outside. He prayed every night for God to replenish his weary spirit and prayed for strength upon rising. Jackson finally realized that Dr. Will would not waver or send him off. They relaxed into life. They blended together like old friends. Will didn't want the stigma the boy might have previously associated with fathers, and it was obvious that Jackson would have passionately resisted to the idea. Will wasn't concerned with labels; he considered himself the boy's guardian and supported the independent youth from just outside his radar.

TABUK, SAUDI ARABIA

Religious leader and militia leader, Pirum Hami, waves then sends a stiff fist into the air as he finalizes his speech about concurring the devil in all of his form with unwavering will and as much aggressive force as needed. He spoke of tactics, new weapons, and guarding the Saudi's will with an iron fist as symbolized by his own fist still firm in the dusk air. He bellowed "With an iron fist" once more from the pit of his guts, and the five hundred plus militia soldiers hollered accordingly while shoving their own fists into the air. He turned and smiled satisfied to his colleagues behind him on the balcony. Jahem Reah and Timus Apon held flat effects on sun-darkened faces buried under thickets of untamed beards and mustaches. They had been highly honored by leader Pirum Hami for over fifteen years and had proved themselves by lack of fear, questions, and conscious.

Standing on his left was his family. His wife, Dei Luna, was an attractive, respected woman and had a hard kindness in her. She supported her husband in her words and actions but pretended to be blind to his hate and distorted perceptions of evil. She didn't have his ear or his heart. She played the role; she knew no other life; and he would allow her no other life. With his blessings, she would work to start charities; it was the only thing that gave her peace. She wondered how many empty stomachs she would have to feed or orphans she would have to house and dress to pay for her husband's sins.

Next to Mama Dei were their sons—all four lined by size and all wearing the same militia uniform as their father—the same uniform of the storms of troops outside, which were now marching off. Pirum looked admiringly at them. They were strong, handsome, and had adopted the same black will as their father—a will detached of emotion and void of freedom. Thamus, twenty-three; Paul, twenty-two; Nomih, twenty-one; and Brunal, nineteen were all unknowing prisoners of the world around them and of their father.

Last was Sonih. She was fifteen years old and the most beautiful young woman around, but she wore her beauty like an old scar. She did not flaunt it. In fact, unless directly reminded of it, she would forget it altogether. She turned and walked off the balcony in open defiance of her father. He turned to the fading soldiers for one last wave and to see if anyone had noticed his daughter's behaviors. They all filed off the balcony, and Pirum, filled with rage, yelled his daughter's name. When she failed to turn, stop, or even recognize that anyone was talking, Pirum ran up to her and pushed her against the wall of the stairway.

"Mind your behaviors, child," he taunted at her. "If you're not with us, Sonih," and as he deeply threatened her, his grip on the shoulder tightened. Sonih turned once more and made a slow, defiant gait toward the exit.

Moments later, Sonih found her pace quickening until her movements exploded into a full sprint. She felt the vibration of footsteps beside her and stopped abruptly. She arrived at her destination—a park, which once upon a time, had been her haven. She hadn't remembered the rusty, broken swings or the dry, dusty ground in her childhood dreams. Now she returned to this lost and lonely park out of habit, hoping to find the peace that it once had brought her. But her strength was not here; subconsciously she knew it had never been here. She lost her strength two years ago, and a lonely guilt burned her deep inside. She closed her eyes and lay on the dusty ground behind overgrown weeds, which hid her. She could feel her—still here, like the phantom pain of a severed leg. She ached for comfort, but the uneasy chaos of her mind only grew throughout the years.

"Korih," Sonih softly whispered. With the sound of her name, tears ran down Sonih's face. *Korih was so much stronger than me*, Sonih thought to herself.

She was her best friend, companion, and identical twin sister. Korih was outspoken, wild-spirited, and possessed a limitless heart. She was Sonih's true comfort, but she was debrided from the group and from the world.

Two years, one month, and thirteen days, Sonih thought as she replayed the images like an old movie burned forever in her mind.

They woke early that day; they were going to make a difference and "not like Mama Dei," they'd tell themselves.

"We have to stand up, Sonih," Korih would preach. "We have to know we tried. That the world didn't fall in all around us and we sat by pretending that we didn't see it."

Korih would inspire. So in an act of opposition, they photocopied hundreds of letters preaching against their father's policies and the violence that often accompanied. It argued not to let one more life be lost due to the directionless pride of the power-hungry. They rode their bikes through three villages, handing out flyers and stuffing them into mailboxes and under doors. When they arrived back home, it was nine o' clock that night, and the dusk was heavy. Their eyes met briefly, and they took a deep breath before they pushed open the front door. They walked up the stairs with shoulders touching and a strong, daring gaze. The door at the top of the stairs opened, and their father stood silently waiting for his daughters. His stare was flat and detached. The girls stopped at the top of the stairs when they reached their father. He looked the young girls in the eyes and placed a hand on each of their shoulders. Pirum yelled furiously and forced forward with all his might and hurdled the girls backward down the long flight of cement stairs—their terrified screams interrupted by each thud on the stairs. Their bodies met on the landing, broken and bleeding. They had no words; they hadn't enough breath to allow for words. Korih's hand found Sonih's, as they both faded into unconsciousness. When Sonih awoke, she was alone, in a local hospital. The pain screaming through her body was none to that which tormented her mind and soul. Korih's death certificate read that death was the result of injuries sustained during an accidental fall, and nobody challenged it. Sonih's mom remained captive within her own realities. Sonih's hope had become like a ghost; her life was like a fog.

LOOKING FOR ANSWERS

Jenna sat reading her book, until Alan's truck turned the corner of their street. She quickly jumped up and raced over to the computer. He had pleaded to her with concerning eyes to let this new development with Thomas go.

"What he needs is stability," Alan would urge.

She typed *sayshea* in the Google search—*saishea, saishia*—nothing. Alan had only run to a nearby convenience store, and her time was marked. Desperately, she typed *saishiea*, and she gasped as pages of results appeared before her. She clicked each on the selections and printed. She folded the unread papers and put them behind Thomas's picture in the frame and put it back on the hook, as Alan's headlights turned into the drive.

Jenna waited nearly one week before an opportunity came to read the curious papers. Alan forced a moist kiss on Jenna and grabbed her up in his arms and swayed her back and forth before easing her feet back on the ground.

"Are you sure you're OK with me playing poker tonight?" Alan quizzed.

"Of course, I don't care," Jenna consoled him. "You play every week. You always have a good time."

She tried to numb her face, but she knew he could see her.

"You've just been quiet lately, acting a little differently. Is everything OK?" Alan inquired.

Jenna's mind whirled. She wanted to tell him about the papers that were hidden—about searching the internet, despite his pleas, about her fears and curiosity. Guilt flooded her as she denied his questioning and gave him one more reassuring hug.

This is my soul mate, Jenna thought to herself as he pulled out of the drive. *Why would I sacrifice even one ounce of trust in our sacred marriag?* Jenna self-assessed.

Jenna's heavy heart lifted slightly as Thomas laughed innocently at his perceptions of the world around him. His eyes found Jenna's eerily and were steady and persistent for ten seconds.

"Saishiea," the child bellowed again.

Her hair stood up again at the sound and due to the fact that Thomas rarely made eye contact, let alone for a steady ten seconds. The word sounded different from the moans or babble that was common to Thomas. She recovered the hidden papers and began reading. Jenna's mouth dropped open, and she deeply gasped. A paralyzing breath held her until a conscious realization allowed her to breathe normally again. She felt her heart pound deeply as she read.

ACCIDENTAL FIRE CLAIMED THE LIFE OF SEVEN was the heading. It continued on to say that in the region of Hail, Saudi Arabia, a well-established restaurant in Shaisheiea—by the name of Shaishiea's hope—caught fire.

"The accidental explosion was thought to be caused by a gas leak in the kitchen. Many patrons escaped with mild cases of smoke inhalation," Jenna read to herself as her vision tunneled. She struggled to comprehend the situation she found herself in. "Germany mourns as two government officials vacationing in the area were killed in the blaze," Jenna read on silently. "No foul play suspected," was echoed throughout the article as she read perplexed as to how this distant disaster could possibly affect her family.

She looked to her son, expecting answers but only finding babbles and jerky movements.

"Were we supposed to stop this, Tommy?" she quizzed anxiously, but the child was undisturbed by her outburst and only sloppily slobbered as he gnawed at his fist. She retreated to the humble solitude of the bathroom and dropped to her knees to pray.

"Am I going crazy?" she inquired but felt no answers through the noise in her mind.

She paced the time away until Alan returned from playing cards. Thomas was long since in bed, and Jenna sat snuggled in her chair looking beyond the TV, trying to find peace within herself. Alan slid through the door and quickly flooded Jenna with kisses. They both laughed, and for a minute she was still. She was only in that moment—overwhelmed by the feel of his kisses.

The chapping wind of reality blew through her again, but she refused the only shelter she had known.

"I know I've been acting strangely, Alan. I've let this whole thing with Thomas go too far. I think I just need to get away for a few days and relax. Would you care if I went to my sisters this weekend?" Jenna suggested softly.

Jenna's sister, Holly, lived in Chicago. Alan's smile never wavered, and he pulled Jenna to him.

"Sounds good," Alan whispered. "Under one condition," Alan laughed seductively, and he pulled Jenna from her chair.

As they walked with arms intertwined, he interjected, "Me and Tommy can have a man's weekend." Alan bragged.

Jenna quickly interrupted him. "Thomas's coming with me," Jenna blurted.

She heard the shortness of what she had said and tried to soften the statement with a reassuring smile.

"Why would he go with you, if you're trying to relax?" Alan inquired.

"My sister hasn't seen Thommy in months, she wouldn't have me visit without him," Jenna explained.

Jenna's statement brought an uneasy look to Alan's rugged face. Then he smiled back at her acceptingly.

"Whatever," Alan added playfully.

MISSION TRIP

The hint of fall was in the air. Hellbound filled his lungs with the cool crispness of the German night air. He and the doctor made their way home from a celebratory dinner at an elite restraint in the area.

"I can't believe you graduated," repeated Will on the jeep ride home.

Hellbound was at the wheel—the first time and maybe last Will would hand over the keys of his pride and joy. The light from the streetlight reflected off the new yellow paint job the doctor had treated himself to upon completion of the research at the university. Hellbound looked back with a familiarly cocky smile.

"Don't seem so surprised, Will," Hellbound teased.

The silence was interrupted again by the buzzing of Will's cell phone.

"This thing drives me crazy," he complained. "I should've left it at home."

"Just answer it," witted the arrogant teenager.

"No, I'm not going to ruin my evening gabbing on the phone," Will rebuked.

They walked into their home, and immediately the answering machine taunted Will. The number 10 was flashing in bright-red lights.

"Someone wants to talk to me," Will laughed.

Hellbound shook his head knowingly. Six messages were left by Dr. Abner, who pleaded with Will to call—that an emergency had come up. When Dr. Harrington quickly returned his call, he learned that Matt Abner's wife had gone into premature labor and he was unable to go overseas to lead the charity mission planned by the university.

"I've got public lectures planned all week," Will informed him, knowing full well that Dr. Abner's emergency preceded his own. "OK, I'll handle it," Will reassured him. "You just take care of your wife, and don't worry about work," Will added before he hung up the phone. Will's face was frozen in a pale stare.

"What's wrong?" Hellbound asked three times before Will's blank stare was interrupted.

"Dr. Abner was assigned to lead this huge charity mission to help feed the needy. His wife went into preterm labor, and now he can't go. That leaves me, head of the psychiatry board, to fill in the hole. The huge problem is that with all the new research finds, the university has got me doing three public lectures next week alone. You know how huge these events are. I can't miss them," Will emphasized his dilemma.

Hellbound nodded his head sympathetically. Then the teen burst out, "I almost forgot I've got a date tonight!"

"This date won't end the way your last did!" the doctor scolded sternly.

"Why, are you going to be in your bed?" Hellbound spoke with cocky sarcasm.

Will was still taken, at times, by the blunt way the young man spoke regardless of atmosphere and etiquette.

"Is she on my staff?" Will firmly inquired.

A surprised look passed the young man's face briefly.

"Don't give me that look. She better not be on my staff. Do you know how awkward that is?" Will scolded.

"One administrative assistant and I'm forever getting interrogated before any date," Hellbound sounded annoyed.

"She was a good assistant," the doctor stressed.

"I think you liked her," Hellbound teased as Will rolled his eyes unamused. "Anyway, can I use the jeep for a few hours?" Hellbound's voice deepened.

The doctor needed not speak. The amused smile on his face let Hellbound know that the notion was an impossibility. The doctor retreated for the night, and Hellbound quickly confirmed the date on his phone, and soon his run-down Ford Torres paced out of the drive.

Dr. Harrington's night passed slowly and was filled by nagging pleas to every staff member he could think of. The excuses varied, but the apologetic declines all the same, as though they had been rehearsed. Will fell to sleep with a headache but arose hours later with an idea. He stumbled his way to his feet in the darkness. The clock read four. He pushed into Hellbound's room, briefly forgetting Hellbound's adult privacy through the brilliance of his own idea. The room was empty. Will mazed himself through the house and found Hellbound bent over leaning into an open refrigerator. The doctor chuckled at the memories of all the midnight rummages through out the years.

"You can do it," Will burst out excitedly.

Hellbound stood up and spun around at the startle of Will's voice.

"What are you talking about?" Hellbound inquired.

"The charity trip—it would look great when applying to college or jobs, you could see another piece of this world, help the poor, and show me how responsible you can be," Will explained.

The doctor's smile was frozen in time, waiting for Hellbound's response.

"OK," Hellbound responded without much deep consideration. "Where?" the teen inquired between bites of a sandwich.

"Saudi Arabia. You leave on Monday," Will answered.

Hellbound finished the last bite of his sandwich, downed half a glass of water, and started moving toward his bedroom.

"Good night, Will," Hellbound spoke and flashed an empty smile at Will as he passed by.

"Good night, bud. See ya tomorrow," Will spoke softly.

He was still taken back by how indifferent Hellbound was. Will had hoped to see at least a hint of excitement. Now Will's mind reconsidered the offer and toiled around all that could go wrong. He exhaled deeply while quietly reminding himself of the bind he had been in.

I didn't have a choice, the doctor thought to himself. *This is the best option, considering.* Will's thoughts struggled to justify the newly growing worries that filled his mind—eventually finding a temporary peace within himself and retreating back to bed for the remainder of the night.

The weekend moved quickly between getting an emergency passport, packing, and going through all Dr. Abner's trip plans.

"Good news, Hellbound. The cargo plane has room for your car. You can take it so you can go into town after the day's end or go sightseeing."

The teen acknowledged Will with a nod of his head.

"We've got to go meet the team in a few minutes. What are you going to wear?" Will questioned.

Hellbound looked at his attire and back at the doctor with surprise.

"What's wrong with this?" Hellbound responded, looking down at his torn jeans.

"You're going to be the youngest one going, and you're in charge. I just want you to look a little more professional so the team will be more comfortable," the doctor coaxed.

"They're going to be uncomfortable regardless of what I wear, Doc," Hellbound reasoned.

An hour later, they found themselves at the airport, wandering through a cargo plane that was bigger than Hellbound had imagined. Crates of food and clothing were stacked nearly to the ceiling and consuming over half of the plane's storage space. The pilot directed Hellbound to the area where his car would be secured down. When Will and Hellbound exited the ramp, they noticed people were arriving and beginning to gather excitedly around the plane.

"Hello, everyone. I'm Dr. Harrington, and this is my colleague, Jackson, who will be leading this mission."

The volunteers nodded with big smiles and introduced themselves. Most were from area churches, a few from the Red Cross, and one was a student volunteer. Hellbound walked down the ramp and shook each hand, requesting names and offering his own name.

"I'm Jackson, but some call me Hellbound," Hellbound introduced himself.

A heavyset woman that appeared to be in her sixties gasped and took her husband's arm nervously. Her husband smiled and offered Hellbound his hand.

"I supposed I've been called worse." The long, furry man snickered at his own words, and Hellbound firmly accepted his handshake. "I'm James, and this is my wife, Dee," the man added kindly.

They mingled and reviewed the mission plan for about an hour.

"I want to see everyone back at six sharp tomorrow morning," Hellbound smiled, waved, and gestured to Dr. Harrington that he was ready to go.

Will was overwhelmed by Hellbound's intensity again, but this time it was somewhat comforting.

The morning came quickly, and Hellbound welcomed it. He knew his guardian's passions—working with troubled youth, his jeep, and sleep. Will dreaded the mornings and slept deeply. So Will was oblivious to the fact that Hellbound had woken early that day and crept quietly into the doctor's room and turned off his obnoxious alarm. Will made a point of emphasizing the importance of seeing him off at the airport the night prior. Hellbound, though, had other intensions.

Much later, Will woke refreshed and immediately knew he had overslept. He gasped at the sight of nine fifty-three on the clock. Will jumped to his feet and raced through the house in a panic. Will was mildly relieved, and then he found a note sketched on the back of scrap paper. His eyes jumped over the words, and altogether he crumpled the paper and ran out into the driveway. He yelled curses from the pit of himself. He walked down the drive in only his boxer shorts and turned to inspect the back of Hellbound's car. His bright-yellow jeep was gone, just as the note told.

"Sorry, Doc, my car can barely handle the freeway, let alone the desert. Don't worry, I'll baby it."

Will remembered the mocking words in the note before turning red with rage and stomping back into the house.

Half a day later, Hellbound landed half a world away, in the desert city of Tabuk. The team exited the cargo plane and entered the chaotic hurry of the busy town. Harsh noises danced around their heads. They regrouped, and Hellbound signaled the team.

"These crates need to be unloaded ASAP," Hellbound directed.

He found a mechanical lift and wheeled it to one of the larger males in the group. He directed the group to the flatbed trucks that had assembled and gave each man a station. Forty minutes later, Hellbound herded the crew into the three flatbed trucks.

"We'll drop off the trucks at the warehouse and then settle into our motel rooms," Hellbound informed.

The teen ran aboard the cargo plane and drove off minutes later in a mint-yellow jeep. It was as out of place in this setting as the crew that had brought it. Thirty miles later, they had secured the truck in a large vacant warehouse and were resting and snacking—in a hotel that was near ruins. Most of the crew came to Hellbound, assertively voicing their disapproval with the hotel.

"We're close, people. We'll save an hour of day light every day by staying here. Besides, we're here to work, not to lounge about the hotel. I'm sorry if you were under the impression this was a vacation. Now I have to go meet with our local volunteers. I'll see everyone up and ready at five tomorrow morning," Hellbound bluntly reasoned. He didn't attempt to dodge the crew's condemning looks as he jumped into the jeep and sped off.

He arrived at the building an hour later, after being lost nearly half of the trip by confused signs and unfamiliar numbering. He rapped deeply on the solid wood door. Moments later, the metal peephole slid open and revealed part of a woman's face. She mumbled something in her foreign tongue that Hellbound couldn't understand, and the metal cover of the peephole slid back shut. Hellbound stood for a few minutes and began knocking again. He had turned to leave when the door abruptly swung open and a woman with a warm smile invited him in. She spoke some very broken German. They sat at a table in the next room, which was already set up for tea. She urged him to sit.

"They call me Mama Dia," the woman introduced herself, and with these words, she offered him a cup of tea.

He grabbed the cup firmly and rested it back on the table. "They call me Hellbound," the young man replied.

Her face changed to one of confusion. "You are Dr. Abner?" she questioned, struggling with her words.

"Dr. Abner couldn't come. I'm here in his place," Hellbound spoke slowly to try to help with understanding.

"Hellbound?" she confirmed with broken emphasis on each syllable.

With an acknowledging nod from the teen, her face changed to that of confusion again. They confirmed the times and the numbers of volunteers for the relief mission before Hellbound excused himself to leave. Before Hellbound had made it to the door, it swung open. A group of several young Saudi men pushed in, dressed in stiff blue uniforms. Shined brass buttons lined down the front of their jackets. Hellbound noticed their harsh expressions and felt the unstable energy in the room rise. Mama Dia raced over between Hellbound and the newcomers. Her hard-soled heels clunked at an uneasy pace.

"These sons," she spoke brokenly; her voice cracked briefly before she gently cleared her throat.

She smiled at Hellbound, but her sons stood frozen like statues.

"You're German," the eldest son, Thamus, interjected.

"I'm Hellbound," Hellbound spoke with an easy tongue and held himself with a relaxed, unchanged stance. Hellbound smiled mockingly at her son, not expecting one in return.

"Aren't they all? Aren't all Germans hell-bound?" Mama Dia's youngest son, Brunai, spoke with an instigating tone.

The soldiers all broke into brief laughter and then let their cold stares fall back on their guest.

"Not the ones bringing relief to your people."

Hellbound smiled boldly. Mama Dia quickly escorted her guest to the door.

"Six tomorrow at the warehouse," she quickly reviewed. "I bring ten volunteers." She smiled with her mouth, but her eyes spoke of nervousness. "Bye," Mama Dia spoke abruptly before she flashed one last weak smile and then quickly shut the door.

PLAYGROUND

Hellbound left their house, but he didn't go back to the hotel. He drove a few miles away and parked at the entrance to a small store. He found a bottle of water and a chicken pita and decided to walk through the town. He followed an alley that led to an open field. He pushed through the field, taking in the landscape. As he wandered aimlessly to the town, he noticed the outline of objects in the distance. He moved toward the objects as he finished his pita. He now recognized the objects as a playground and sat down at the base of an old slide. He relaxed back into the slide's form and breathed in the last of the dry day. The sun now began to fade from the pale sky. Suddenly, an intruder burst into park. She laughed quietly to herself as she halted her sprint. She leaned back to fill her lungs before she noticed Hellbound's presence. She gasped in startle, and then she giggled quietly, trying to quickly replay her behaviors. Her brow was softened with sweat from her sprint. She wore the loose, colorful wrap custom to her country. Hellbound sat frozen, his mind whirled in disorientation. She looked through him. He felt a vulnerable ache burn deep inside himself. She moved with the slow grace of the calm evening wind and sat Indian style on the ground in front of his feet. She looked to the ground for moments before connecting again with his eyes. Hellbound was overcome by a comforting peace. He smiled humbly but made no attempt to speak. Her dark eyes were genuine and pure. She sat in front of him, for minutes, discovering him with her eyes, as if she could feel the story of his life unfolding before her. She stood with a familiar, simple grace and walked beyond him. She stopped six feet away but didn't turn. Hellbound jumped to his feet and turned to face her. His heart was beating against his sternum as if it were trying to break out. She turned around briefly and looked daringly back at him. Then she took off in the same sprint that had brought her here. Without thinking, he sprinted after her. Her long, dark hair danced as she dodged through the park equipment. They laughed with the innocence of children at play. Finally, they cascaded into an open field where Hellbound used his long strides to catch her. She stopped running at the gentle pressure of his warm hand on her shoulder. She turned and saw him. She softly touched his cheek with the sweaty palm of her hand. He closed his eyes and turned into her hand. After a moment, he felt her hand glide away. He kept his eye shut tightly, trying to savor the warm imprint on his cheek as it slowly faded. By the time he opened his eyes, she had distanced herself a half of a field from him. She didn't look back. She just slowly pushed through the tall grass toward town.

2019.11.27

RELIEF

The next morning, before the sun broke beyond the horizon, the charity team had already assembled and boarded the bus. Hellbound followed in the jeep, leaving them only for minutes to stop off and get coffee for the crew. He glanced at his cell phone for the first time. "Five forty" was found at the bottom on the tiny screen; across the middle read fourteen new messages. Hellbound knew the majority of these were probably from Will, and he snapped the phone shut slowly, letting it slide into his pocket. He unlocked the warehouse door and pushed the old barn-style sliding doors apart. The pallets of nonperishables seemed to tower higher than he remembered. He quickly assigned his team the tasks of separating the pallets, assembling varied food into boxes, and setting up tables and chairs. The bus of home volunteers arrived at six exactly. Mama Dia was the first to emerge from the bus. She was followed silently by eight other women, who seemed to be of similar social status as Mama Dia. Mama Dia lined her volunteers up and began introducing them as the last volunteer filtered off the bus.

Hellbound heard nothing of what Mama Dia said as she approached him. He only saw beyond her. He was overcome with the whirlwind of emotions of the night before. Hellbound was suddenly grounded from the broken mumble of Mama Dia's formal introductions to the familiar newcomer.

"That's my daughter, Sonih," Mama Dia explained with a grimaced expression on her face. "She is wild in her youth. She still mourns for her sister." Mama Dia spoke as her own face faded to sadness, revealing her own loss. "She won't be trouble," Mama Dia reassured with a slow, broken tongue.

The woman next to Mama Dia took her arm in comfort. Hellbound quickly dispersed the new help to their designated areas as Mama Dia proceeded to explain to them their jobs.

The woman-child disappeared behind a pallet, pretending to be absorbed by the new environment. Hellbound routed himself through the team and around the other side of the pallet. He peeked around the back to find her waiting, with her back leaning easily against the boxed foods. She smiled shyly without looking toward him. He forced his way into her gaze for recognition and spoke softly.

"Sonih?" Hellbound asked.

Sonih matched his slow, soft voice and moved into his space.

"Yes, my name's Sonih. I don't know your name, but you're familiar to me. I can feel your spirit as if it talks to me," Sonih confessed.

Her fluent words paralyzed him, and with a helpless urge, he quickly pulled her face to his own. They kissed deeply, without fear of consequences, without comprehension of the world around them. When they parted, she smiled innocently at him—her eyes still blazed with passion. Sonih dropped the tight grasp of his hand and let it fall back to his side. She walked away with a simple grace that intoxicated him. She spent the morning working at the station, filtering through the herds of needy people, who partook of the charity. Hellbound moved about, troubleshot the weak areas, and filled in when demand was shown. The lunch hour came and went, and the staff began requesting breaks. Hellbound decided to clear out the building and lock up so the chaos of the crowd could die down and the crew could briefly refresh themselves. He locked up the warehouse door as a crew member returned with lunch. The team mingled and laughed and quickly became interested in the customs of the home volunteers. The easy conversation hushed to silence, with the forceful banging on the door and the threatening foreign calls that brought most of the home volunteers uneasily to their feet. Mama Dia urged the key away from Hellbound and raced to the door. She blocked the intruders momentarily with high-pitched pleas and her delicate stance, until she was forced to the side.

Her husband, Pirum, who had a harsh will and unknown intentions, marched into the warehouse. He walked to Hellbound with dark, challenging eyes and confirmed that Hellbound was in charge of this mission. Hellbound was seemingly oblivious to the military consults that stood just behind each shoulder of Pirum or the ten matching soldiers that lined up blocking the exit, as his attention settled on the unstable tyrant before him.

"Yes, I'm in charge," the teen stood and spoke with the selfless courage of a man.

"I don't know if you're aware that Germany has made unfriendly advancement toward Saudi Arabia. All foreign identities affiliated with Germany are going to be held subject to resolving conflicts and assuring there is no alternative motives to this trip," Pirum spoke coldly while he smiled arrogantly. "I'm sure you understand. It's necessary for both our safety," Pirum explained with a sinister tone.

"I can have our jet fueled and people out of here within the hour," the teen assertively interjected.

General Pirum's brows deepened with a forced expiration. "This is not a negotiable. We will move you to a safe location. All that resist will be taken by force," Pirum demanded angrily.

He ended the conversation by flipping the safety off the handgun attached to his hip. He turned his back to the young German and exited the warehouse. The military leaders behind him stayed put and began shouting orders toward the German volunteers. Some of the women from his team began to sob and grab onto each other.

"Don't resist," Hellbound urged the men that accompanied him. "I'm going for help," he whispered while lining up his team.

"You'll be killed," an older woman whispered back to the youth.

"We may be killed regardless," Hellbound suspected to himself.

Hellbound then turned and led the team out of the warehouse, tapping each of their shoulders as they passed him. The soldiers thoroughly patted down the volunteers before they entered the bus.

Hellbound suddenly broke from his team and ran with all his force toward the back parking lot, where the jeep was parked. Shots followed his footsteps as he neared the jeep. He hurdled over the door of the topless jeep and in a single movement put the key in the ignition and was off with off with daring speed. As the jeep squealed down the street, gunshots filled the air. Then the offensive shooting abruptly seized. He glanced back to find Sonih standing in the back, grasping the roll bars and daring them to shoot. The soldiers looked at each other with confusion and jumped into their vehicles in pursuit. Mama Dia stood numb, filled with helplessness.

Sonih jumped into the passenger seat and began shouting directions. Hellbound followed her directions with speed and precision and without hesitation. They wound up parked in a run-down shed on the outskirts of town. They left the jeep and raced cautiously through the forgotten desert.

"I've got an old car parked about five miles from here. If we can get there in an hour, we may have a chance," Sonih suggested.

Hellbound's eyes widened at the consideration of this challenge. They fearlessly pushed through the dry, taunting air. Hellbound felt the tightening strain of his calves as he lunged over the loose, sandy terrain. Sonhi's eyes remained fixed, and she gave no physical clues of fatigue. Their young breathing turned to gasping pants, as the unforgiving sun slowly depleted the couple of needed fluids. She urged him on with her eyes and gestured him to a nearby group of trees.

They approached a faded shell of a car, which was out of place with its surroundings. Sonih forced the door open against the screeching metallic resistance of the deteriorating door and fumbled under the seat for keys. Sonih's breathing turned to wheezes as she fought her body to recover. She clumsily started the car, as Hellbound's body fell limp with exhaustion into the passenger's seat. She drove with determination, as if she dreamed of this escape forever. Hellbound recouped enough to speak.

"How'd you know I'd run? I mean, the jeep. You were there," Hellbound fumbled over his words.

She glanced at him with intense eyes. "I don't know. It's like I know you, somehow," Sonih responded.

With her comment, he smiled at her. "You could make a fierce enemy," he suggested.

She spoke back with innocent laughter. "Or a daring ally," she challenged.

"I know what you mean," Hellbound confessed. "About knowing me—you're familiar to me too, yet mysterious too." He gave into an embarrassed laugh.

The seriousness of the situation caught up to them in a single sobering recognition. Hellbound rediscovered the cell phone from his pocket and selected Will's cell number from speed dial. Before Hellbound could speak, Will answered the phone already halfway through a one-sided argument.

"You selfish son of a bitch, you stole my jeep and betrayed one of the only friends you have in this world and don't even have the balls to answer the goddamn phone!"

Will paused only to catch his breath, but Hellbound took advantage.

"Shut up for one damn second. This is an emergency. The Saudi military captured our volunteers. They said Germany started conflict with them and they have to make sure we're not involved. It's a load of bullshit. I had a feeling this was planned," Hellbound quickly interrupted.

Will struggled to grasp what Hellbound was saying.

"Where? They took our volunteers where?" Will asked fearfully.

"I don't know," Hellbound responded.

Will sputtered guiltily.

"I escaped. I had to get help. I was no good to them there," Hellbound continued.

Will felt empty and helpless. "Where are you now?" Will inquired.

"I don't trust these cell towers," Hellbound responded cautiously.

"Is this for real, Hellbound?" Will confirmed, still overwhelmed by the surreal situation.

"I wish it weren't, Will. This is a bad scene. I'm gonna try like hell to get our people back," Hellbound promised. "Will?" Hellbound confirmed Will's attention.

"I'm coming. We're coming to help," Will interrupted.

"Will," Hellbound's voice deepened and wavered with emotion.

"Hellbound, what is it?" Will urged fearfully.

"I'm pulling the battery out of my phone for now. I don't want any way to track us. What I'm trying to say is, well, if I don't see you again—I mean, you never gave up on me. I did some really bad things, Will…" Hellbound's ramblings faded. "I love you, Will," Hellbound confessed sincerely.

"I know you do, buddy. I love you too. We're coming to help. Just stay put. Don't go back," Will emphasized.

Will felt an emptiness on the line and called Hellbound's name, with a knowing desperation. Will then looked at his own cell phone to confirm the call was disconnected.

2019.11.25

DIVERSION

Jenna called from her sister's house to ease Alan's mind that they had made a safe trip to Chicago.

"I love you, Alan. We'll be home Monday evening," Jenna reassured, ending the call with a heavy heart and hoping Alan hadn't noticed.

Jenna's sister, Kate, returned from the kitchen with a tray of snacks and warm tea. They sat and visited at the table.

"How long have ya got, kiddo?" Kate inquired with a nurturing tone.

"Our overlay was six hours, so we should be back up to O'Hare within four hours," Jenna informed.

"So tell me about this research group that Thomas is a part of," Kate warmly tried to catch up on her sister's affairs.

"Oh, I probably couldn't explain it right. Something about using a natural hormone to help damaged neurons recover and grow," Jenna spoke with an easy tone but ended with a yawn. She hoped Kate would attribute her avoidance of the topic to travel fatigue.

"Well, I thought you were done with all that experimental stuff," Kate inquired.

"We wouldn't be going except Thomas's neurologist prodded and prodded and raved about all the advancements being made. I figured we'd give it one more shot. It's real low risk, anyway," Jenna explained. Jenna nodded in support of what she'd said, and Kate nodded, acknowledging.

"Stanford, right?" Kate confirmed.

"Yeah, Stanford," Jenna sighed.

Alan arrived at work, in Ohio. He filled his "Best Dad in the World" coffee cup that boasted Thomas's picture and proceeded into a quality improvement meeting. He sat next to Philip, an older man and good friend from work.

"Hey, Alan. How's it going?" Philip offered.

"All right," Alan said with a smile.

"Sounds like your family's off for an adventure. Shame you couldn't go," Philip said sincerely.

Alan's eyebrows rose, and he smiled with surprise.

"Chicago?" Alan said abruptly.

"No, Saudi Arabia. Donna works at O'Hare. She mentioned they had booked a flight a few days back," Philip explained.

Alan's smile dropped, and his eyes glazed over. Alan sprung to his feet.

"When?" he demanded with urgency.

"Well, I'm not sure. Soon, I think," Philip fumbled.

Alan raced out the door, knocking down a chair and bumping in to coworkers in the panic of the moment.

Jenna's nervousness heightened as she loaded Thomas back into the rental car.

"Good luck," Kate waved excitedly. "Call me." Kate smiled as she walked back into her house.

Jenna could feel her heart jump with fear and throb with guilt. They proceeded routinely through customs and security check. She waited anxiously for the boarding call, trying to focus on Thomas's care as distraction of her own emotions.

"What am I doing?" Jenna whispered respectively to herself.

"Saishiea," Thomas moaned with eerie timing.

"Your mom's a madwoman, Thomas," she confessed quietly while brushing his hair back with her fingers.

"We will begin boarding international flight 815 to Sakakah, Saudi Arabia. We'll start by loading all handicap or special needs persons," a deep voice echoed through the speakers.

"That's us, kid." Jenna said flatly.

Thomas now fading to sleep, didn't rose for the boarding. A kind flight attendant assisted in getting Thomas's wheelchair fastened securely. Jenna smiled weakly at the attendant as she tightened the last strap. Jenna fumbled a magazine as people were clumsily herded to their seats. Jenna was too consumed by thought to pay attention to the pilot's introduction, the safety presentation, or the cue to buckle up for takeoff.

"They said buckle up," a familiar voice abruptly insisted, pulling Jenna spiraling back to reality.

"Alan," Jenna forced out a small, quivering voice already choked with emotion.

Alan sat in the open window-side seat next to Jenna. Alan was frozen with betrayal as he let his flat stare fall toward the crewman working outside the plane.

Jenna pleaded through soft tears. "I wanted to tell you, Alan. I know I'm probably going crazy, but this is something that I feel I had to do. I know how it sounds, but the only regret I have is not telling you. I'm so sorry, Alan!" Jenna pleaded then looked toward him with hopeful anticipation.

"You were going to take our son around the world, to a dangerous place! When did you plan on telling me, Jenna?" Alan spoke coldly but was too deaf with anger to hear Jenna's stumbling response.

"I have never been so furious in all my life," Alan spoke with a hushed tongue and turned his gaze to Jenna's' warm green eyes. "I had a lot of time to think on the drive up here and during my cavity search in security." Alan's' voice softened, and his mouth twitched with the start of smile, but he didn't give in to it.

Jenna's face grimaced with imagination then quickly recovered into the serious eye contact of an eager listener.

"I mean to say, if you would've told me, I never would've allowed it. I put myself in the position of resistance, without even realizing it. My only intentions have been to keep you and Thomas safe," Alan spoke softly and then looked up to meet Jenna's eyes. "Even from your own deceptions," he added boldly and then went on shaking off her explanations and holding his palm up toward her requesting silence. "I need to say this, Jenna! I'm going to be here for you, even when I don't understand you, but never take my son away from me again!" Alan scolded, and the intensity of his stare deepened as Jenna nodded with shame.

"I've always loved you, Alan. You're the only thing that keeps me grounded," Jenna whispered meekly.

"Apparently, not today," Alan joked through heightened tensions. Alan softly grabbed Jenna's hand as the plane thundered into takeoff.

Jenna vulnerably offered Alan all the research she had acquired within the past months. She told him of the small restaurant in Sakakah, which had become synonymous with disaster. Since the fire in recent months, the restaurant has been vacant with ruin. The town's population had dwindled through chaos and fear as reports of private militia rivalries in the area grew. Jenna informed Alan of her deeper suspicions.

"Back to your old law days, hay?" Alan teased quietly.

Jenna flashed him a devious smile and continued with her explanations. "Well, come to find out two German secret service agents were in that building during the fire. All reports still claim the blaze was accidental, but it just doesn't sit with me. A small restaurant, an area overrun with power-hungry tyrants, and two foreign government agents apparently not trained well enough to escape the explosion." Jenna sighed with exhausted relief and looked to Alan for support.

"Well, what do you plan we do?" Alan inquired with a hint of curiosity.

Jenna's heated ramblings were now hushed, her inadequacies shown through in her somber expression. Alan reflected his situation. He knew he would have to make critical decisions in a place where good and justice could always be compromised and truth often lay silent.

They arrived fourteen hours later in a place that matched Alan's expectations. The airport was crowded and noisy. The buildings were old and in poor repair. The courtyard was overrun with aggressive merchants, boisterously pleading for a sale. Their foreign voices were fast and garbled and made Alan increasingly uneasy. The small family pushed through the herds of busy people, collected their luggage, and made for the exit. Alan signaled an old car, which he presumed to be a taxi, and requested it take the family to a local motel.

The motel was lost amongst the unwelcoming buildings of the city. Alan led his family into the surprising sanctuary of a bland room. After a cleansing sigh, Alan was reborn to a new motive.

"Okay, we'll need a plan," Alan organized his wife.

"The site is only about twenty miles from here, but we stick out like a sore thumb," Jenna reminded.

"Then go get some traditional clothes from the venders around the corner, and I'll leave to investigate around dusk," Alan coaxed.

"What about Thomas?" Jenna spoke in surprise.

Alan was dumbfounded by Jenna's comment. "You're not suggesting we take our young, handicapped son into a place where the only thing we understand is how unbelievably dangerous it is." Alan glared back to Jenna in unbelief as he spoke.

Jenna piped up, "He has some connection to this place, maybe the only way we'll see answers is through him."

Alan's tan completion turned ruddy as he struggled through a few deep breaths, trying to soothe a growing anger. Finally, he retreated to the solitude of the bathroom. Jenna, knowing how much her husband had already compromised, left him to unwind and went to buy clothes from a local vendor. They later reconvened under a renewed energy and purpose.

A whirlwind of fears and regrets overcame both Jenna and Alan, but they would not succumb to them now. They did not acknowledge the faults in each other or themselves; they only considered the next step or leap. The managed to find an agreement with a plan. The family sat in an uneasy, relentless silence, suspended in time that failed to pass.

BREAKAWAY

"We must be almost to Sakakah now," Sonih informed Hellbound as a trance of deep thought swept over her face.

Hellbound didn't need speak a word; his inquiring eyes coaxed her to explain.

"This has not been a real safe place lately, lots of gangs and bombings, and some German agents were killed here awhile back. The people will know my face and will turn me without hesitation, for their own personal gain. And you, well, it will be much worse for you. It is not good to be German here, much less a German associated with the disappearance of the general's only daughter," Sonih updated and then paused to console him with her dark eyes. "We'll have to leave the car at least five miles before we arrive in town."

As she spoke, she boldly grabbed his hand and awaited his response. Hellbound's hand went numb with tingling, and he fought to recapture his senses, his vision tunneled, and he laughed nervously. He briefly entertained the irony of the situation. He had never been awkward with women, never lost himself, and now his thoughts felt clumsy and his body felt weak.

The reality of the situation set back in, as they approached the five-mile drop-off point that Sonih had designated. Sonih forced open the door, and the rusted metal of the door screeched and squealed. Hellbound grabbed her tanned forearm suddenly.

"It's broad daylight. We should wait until dusk to slip into the city," Hellbound suggested.

Sonih considered the obstacles versus the time wasted and closed her eyes briefly in reflection. The newly acquainted team decided to wait for the gray cover of night to make further advancements.

The eastern sky now faded to dusk as the teens maneuvered through the run-down alleys of Sakakah. Sonih quickly realized that her brightly decorated clothes would stand out in such an impoverished town, even a night. Hellbound still wore the distinct clothes of his homeland but with the added attention that his pale complexion brought.

"I know a place we can hide out for the night," Sonih informed her companion through whispered breath.

He trustingly followed her through several more allies and through a back alley door, which was marked only by a dark and faded cross. She fearfully forced the door open, and the pair advanced in. It was dimly lit with a few burning lanterns. At first it seemed empty, but then deep laughter carried through the building. Hellbound followed the voices and held Sonih protectively behind him. Hellbound knocked softly on the door that held the jovial voices. The talking abruptly stopped, and heavy footsteps paced toward the door. The man that opened the door was lean and tall. He wore the traditional clothing of a Middle Eastern priest even though his light skin and dusty auburn hair made it obvious he was foreign.

Sonih pushed through Hellbound and spoke to the group in her foreign tongue. Hellbound felt at ease with their friendly body language, but he still withheld any trust, as he had his whole life. The man then smiled and led the couple to a closet and quickly presented traditional clothing that was as desperate as the town. She thanked the men, or so Hellbound presumed, and turned back to him.

"These men are Christian priests. They have done much good for this place and for me," Sonih sincerely praised the men as she handed Hellbound his clothing.

The priests led them into separate rooms and gestured for them to change, but Hellbound refused to leave his companion despite her naive reassurances of safety.

"This is a holy place. It is not customary or acceptable for single persons to room together," Sonih emphasized.

"Then marry us!" Hellbound spoke boldly and without hesitation.

Sonih felt faint and was flooded with warmth. She felt her heart fall into the pit of her stomach. Her eyes were lost in a haze as she considered the consequences. Hellbound gently grabbed her hands and pulled her around the corner for privacy.

"Sonih, I know you're scared, and I know we're young. There're a million reasons why this is a bad idea, but there's something beyond that, a feeling that in spite of the obstacles that this is right. This may be the only thing in my life that I've ever been truly sure of."

Hellbound then leaned down and held her delicate frame and nestled his face into her dark hair, and he felt tears fall from his eyes for the first time ever. Sonih gently broke free of his loving hold and looked up at him with eyes that were calm and strong. She smiled purely and nodded "yes." She softly grabbed his face and kissed his welcoming lips as if they were home to her.

Sonih pulled Hellbound back around the corner and demanded to their new acquaintance, "Marry us."

The man's face changed suddenly to a nervous smile. "No, I can't, as much as it would honor me. This is not proper. I could get into big trouble if anyone found out," the lean man begged.

Soon the unwavering determination of the young teens led to eventual fall of the missionary priest's resistance, and the group shortly found themselves in a humble and darkened room reciting Christian vows under the dim flicker of a tired lantern.

The untraditional honeymoon was a cramp storage room, which was shelter for the night.

"I'm sorry," said the humble missionary as he lay thin, worn blankets on the ground, arranging lumpy old pillows and trying to make his best effort at a make hap bed. "The town is overrun by poverty and loss," he continued "This is unfortunately the best I can do." The lean man spoke and finished with a weak, apologetic smile.

"It's perfect," Sonih nodded sincerely, still acting as an interpreter for the men.

The couple spent the sleepless night lost in conversation, trying to catch up a lifetime in one night.

"How long can you stay here?" Hellbound asked.

His sobering question pulled Sonih back out of the euphoric dream she had created and abruptly to the dangerous reality that surrounded them.

"You're going back?" Sonih asked the question but already knew the answer. "Mama Dai donated the money for this mission. The missionary has known me since I was young. He knew my sister. He'll hide me here," Sonih ensured Hellbound as her gentle embrace tightened.

They savored each moment they had together, knowing it may be their last. Hellbound left hours before the sun rose. Sonih felt the warm goodbye kiss on her forehead; she clenched her eyes tightly as they filled with tears, not wanting to see him leave. She was left only with fear, pain, and a passionate flood of memories. Ironically, it was the pain in which she silently rejoiced.

"For the infinite heartache," Sonih told herself, "was proof that their love was genuine."

2019.11.28

RESCUE

By the time the sun had risen, Hellbound had already found his way back to the familiar abandoned car and was nearing the back entrance of Tabuk. He had darkened his face and dusty blonde hair with clay and worn the garment he had received at the mission as cover.

Hellbound, who had now penetrated the heart of the city, parked the tired car around the corner from Pirim Hami's home. This is where he had been warmly welcomed by Mama Dai. This is now where he watched the city's poor gather for the scraps from the noon meal. Hellbound pushed his way to the center of the desperate mob, mimicking the hungry pleas of the group with a thirsty and cracking voice. The general's youngest son and military councils quickly threw some bread to the crowds while waving traditionally to the people and reciting the motivating mission statement of the city:

"Honor to those who resist the world and stand together for righteousness."

The men smiled then retreated to a black Lincoln. Hellbound studied the car as he further entangled into the desperate group. As the group began to dissipate, Hellbound scanned the premises for his next move. He noted thick metal gates and a heavy wooden door, each with dressed soldiers in close proximity. Hellbound filtered memories, trying to remember the interior layout of the house. He moved through memories, searching for items he could use, places he could hide, areas that were common to soldiers. Hellbound's memory had always been strong and detailed. He had always read people's subtle quest and explored every situation. This was the result of a traumatic early life, or so Will had told him.

Hellbound found a side door that was hidden from the road. The soldier standing nearby looked even younger than himself, but Hellbound paid note to the gun on his right hip. Hellbound collapsed under the scorching sun and struggled awkwardly to his feet. He kept his face toward the ground and moaned weakly. The young soldier hesitated briefly and then hurried over to investigate the unusual behavior. Hellbound, still looking toward the ground, felt the grasp of the soldiers hand on his upper arm in an attempt to steady him. With windlike movements, Hellbound pushed the entire force of his knee into the soldier's abdomen. Before the soldier could react, Hellbound punched with a quick, solid movement, hitting the soldier's temple and causing him to waver and fall into unconsciousness. Hellbound confiscated the soldiers clothes, putting the uniform on himself and taking his old clothes and the soldier underwear and disposing of them after entering the house. Hellbound knew their modest customs would hinder attempts to leave the wooded area and the doors position would hinder other soldiers from hearing him.

He moved through the immaculate house, exploring the boundaries of his memories while avoiding the heavy sounds of the soldier's boots pacing the quarters. He raced up the wooded stairway undetected and hurried into the first empty room. He placed his back against the wall, allowing only moments to slow his pounding heart and heavy breathing. Suddenly, he heard the familiar, high-pitched click of high heels and the opening and shutting of a nearby door. Hellbound left the safety of the vacant room and sprinted lightly, following the ting of the heels against the old wooden floors. Hellbound pushed through the doorway, and Mama Dai's head whipped around in surprise. With a startled look, she started to scold the soldier before realizing who the intruder was. Before Mama Dai could scream, Hellbound covered her mouth with a strong hand. With growing intensity in his eyes and voice, Hellbound firmly demanded she take him to the captive volunteers. She tried to speak, but only soft muffled hums managed to pass her guarded lips.

"A car," the young man demanded.

Mama Dai compliantly pulled for the door, but Hellbound redirected their efforts to the window. The immense brick house was covered with vines. Mama Dai's eyes widened at the silent suggestion. The pair managed out the window and tested the strength of the covering vines.

Some of the dried vines broke free of the old brick house about ten feet up; they caused Mama Dai to lose her grip, fall to the ground, and tumble awkwardly. Hellbound hurried down behind her and jumped quickly to the ground to retrieve her. He pulled Mama Dai to her feet. She tried to reclaim composure by straightening her dress and brushing the dirt and grass from her clothes and hair. They then crept along the barren side of the house, which was void of doors and soldiers. They pushed through some rough brush and on to the nearby street. Hellbound's pace quickened toward his awaiting car, pulling Mama Dai in tow. Compliantly and quietly she followed, showing no hint of fear or anger. Hellbound forced the rusted door open and urged Mama Dai into the car. He noticed a few new cuts on her leg as she pulled them in the car. The blood slowly trickled down her legs, but her face remained void of emotion. Hellbound understood the emptiness. The emptiness was home to him, but he had never felt the same loss in another.

"My Sonih?" she tried her best to plead for her daughter's well-being through the confines of her language barrier.

Hellbound nodded reassuringly and stated, "Yes, Sonih is good."

Mama Dia nodded in a grateful understanding and grabbed Hellbound's forearm.

Hellbound hardened his gaze and narrowed his eyes on Mama Dai as he began drilling her for the location of his team. She flatly directed him through the faded town. Her vulnerable expression turned to him, and she challenged him with her broken words.

"I'll take you to them. Your anger is not necessary," she spoke with unwavering poise.

"Do I scare you?" Hellbound spoke, airing the prideful arrogance of his youth.

"I don't know fear." Mama Dai's words were harsh and then softened with explanation, "When you have nothing to lose, there is nothing to be feared," she explained.

"Your family. Your life," Hellbound suggested with an unthreatening sarcasm.

"Neither of these are mine," she clarified. "Nothing," she repeated with growing certainty.

"Sonih," he inquired naively.

Mama Dai's eyes showed surprise with the sound of her name. Her eyes closed hard, and then she looked at him helplessly. She clenched her chest with both hands.

"My daughters are gone. I feel a burn through me. The pain is unmatched. It follows me and gives me no rest. It is the only thing left for me. I have failed them, and I have failed my God. I fear no death and no man," she emphasized and then continued to blurt out directions.

He drove in silence and felt a careful awareness of something beyond himself, beyond his comprehension. Mama Dai reached her hand outright and pointed toward and old cement building. The building was falling apart but encircled with a much newer barbed wire fence.

The rest of his group was inside the unsanitary confines of the building's basement. This was a facility Pirum Hami had used for all his unofficial conquests. The jail in the basement was made of the block walls that were thinly covered by a dark mold. The mold was consequently tormenting a majority of the mission group, by causing frequent sneezing—red, draining eyes and heavy, wheezy breathing. The immovable bars were steel and ran deep into the block fortress. The mission group clung together and prayed with the exception of a few men who paced their confines like the desperate track of caged tigers. Hami's soldiers came and left with no consistency, showing little doubt in their faith of the prison's strength. The soldiers joked with each other lightheartedly in their native tongue while flipping through their paperwork, giving only an occasional glance at their prisoners.

The click of Mama Dai's solid heels echoed as she entered the basement, bringing both soldiers to attention. Inquiring looks overcame their faces as they began to question why she had come. The prisoners were still now. Some were in a disturbed euphonium. The room tunneled and sound muffled as if they were watching a movie. Mama Dai demanded the soldiers' weapons, but they declined. The soldiers, still lost in confusion, felt the snap of heavy handcuffs on their hands. Hellbound snapped another pair of metal cuffs on the soldiers' opposite legs. By now they had reached for their guns, but their movements were awkward; and unable to catch themselves, the soldiers tumbled forward. The guns slid across the cold cement ground, and Mama Dai ran to claim them. Hellbound joined the tangled soldiers and frisked them quickly for the keys. The soldiers managed to land several punches on Hellbound before he retrieved the keys. The punches slowed Hellbound's efforts but were not damaging due the soldiers limited movements. Without hesitation, Hellbound freed the volunteers.

The group jumped in victory, and smiles filtered through out them. Hellbound and a few other men hurried to calm the rest of the group, reminding them that their "escape was not yet complete." Mama Dai and Hellbound snaked back through the winding prison. The prison's exit opened to the same barren desert field by which they had entered. This time, though, the field's length had been multiplied by the penetrating fear of the moment. Hellbound and Mama Dai waved the group out of the prison and directed them through the field. The group moved in unison to the pace of its slowest member, Deidra. She was heavy, busty, and was in her early sixties. Her unconditioned body struggled for air as she pushed beyond her physical limitations. The firm escort of her husband, Jim, and another sturdy male member of the group helped Deidra to compensate for her lacking speed and strength. They raced halfway across the barren field. Hellbound's deep voice cracked in the dry desert heat as he pleaded with the group to hurry. Suddenly, Hellbound was paralyzed by the sound of heavy tires racing through the loose desert sand. The rusted jeep neared the fleeing prisoners. Hellbound felt as if he was watching the scene through the distant fog of a dream. He felt the vibrating force of his voice yelling escape commands to his group but felt removed from its context. He felt the rapid pounding of his boots in the shifting sand but felt captive to their movements. The jeep quickly bolted in front of the missionary prisoners, readily barricading their escape and leaving them in a cloud of dust. The sting of the dirt against their face slowly faded, and it began to settle heavily in their lungs.

Two men jumped from the jeep, furiously waving guns at the group in an attempt to contain the prisoners. They yelled demands in their native tongue. The group froze in terror. Mama Dai pushed through, to the front of the group, and challenged the foreign soldiers in an equally threatening tone. The soldiers were caught off guard by the familiar voice and panicked to reason with her. They failed to heed to the commands of Mama Dai and began yelling back at her. Mama Dai stood strong at the front of the prisoners with her arms protectively outstretched. One soldier overwhelmed with frustrations raised his gun above his head, and with surge of speed and strength, he struck Deidra on the temple. Her husband lunged at the soldier as Deidra's body felt limp to the ground. In an emotionless show of dominance, the same soldier swung his gun around and pointed it squarely at Deidra's husband, Jim. Mama Dai forced herself between the men and screamed with fury as the gun discharged. Mama Dai and Deidra's husband fell forward on the soldier, and he rolled respectively, trying to wiggle free under their weight. Hellbound sprinted toward the downed soldier with a surge of adrenaline. The power of his kick against the soldier's cheek caused the soldiers head to fall unconscious back to the sandy ground with a heavy thump. The time it took for Hellbound to retaliate an offense was ample enough to allow the second soldier to intervene. The second soldier windmilled his gun around and snapped it precisely into alignment with Hellbound's back. It took a split second before Hellbound realized he was wide open for fire. Hellbound held his breath with regret when he heard the metallic click of the trigger. The cold sound sent a series of chills down his spine, but he spun around with the realization that he was still alive. The gun had jammed. Hellbound punched through the man with a stiff left jab that caused the man to stumble to keep his balance. While the soldier staggered unsteadily from the blow, Hellbound quickly yanked the barrel free of his grasp. The soldier lunged forward to reclaim his weapon before being knocked to the ground by the blunt butt of the gun. The soldier crawled disoriented away from his attacker before lying belly down in the dirt and placing his palms behind his head in surrender.

The surviving prisoners hurried to the aid of their wounded peers. Deidra, her husband, and Mama Dai lay dead because of their injuries. Hellbound felt the helpless burn of sorrow deep in his sole and yelled with an emotional rage, "EVERYONE INTO THE JEEP!"

With hesitance, the remaining eight-member group pulled themselves weeping from their fallen comrades. They piled into the topless jeep—crammed onto each other's laps, on the side of the jeep, and some even standing up on the bumper, holding onto the roll bars. The jeep ride was silent. Some of its riders were still frozen by the traumatic events they'd survived, and some were quiet with fear for the perceived events yet to come. Hellbound sympathetically ached for Sonih's unknown loss. He wanted to be with her and convey to her how brave her mother had been—how she had saved them by her selfless acts of protection. He wanted to hold her. Hellbound retraced the desolate route back to Sakakah as he had done less than twenty-four hours earlier.

2019.11.28

RAMBAGE

Only hours after Hellbound parted from Sonih for his rescue attempt in Tabuk, word spread through Sakakah about a violent raid headed by the Hami Regime. The tall chaplain pleaded with Sonih to run, knowing that his modest home was no longer a place of refuge but rather the most suspected cover for the missing Hami girl.

"Where should I go?" Sonih pleaded. "Nowhere is safe for me," Sonih concluded.

The kind chaplain fell silent, and a lost look appeared in his eyes. She sensed his fear and saw his eyes grow glossy and red as he fought back tears.

"I have failed you, child," the man's voice was weak and cracking with emotion.

His head was bowed, and his other workers hurried to cover up any evidence that they had a guest the night before. Suddenly, the man looked up and spoke with a spirit of hope. He explained that a once-thriving bar was now abandoned following a suicide bombing attempt by a local man. He described the trash and wastes that now littered the broken structure, which may work as a temporary cover. Sonih slipped out the back window and wandered through the town, staying close to the cover of homes and alleys. She was dressed in the traditional clothes of a Middle Eastern man, hoping to avoid a second glance by militia. She found the remains of the building at the edge of town just as her friend had described. She was immediately overwhelmed by the foul smells of human waste and rotting food. She walked along the outer walls of the building, stepping over trash, trying not to disturb any of the remains or leave any suspicion of human presence. She tucked herself behind the building in a narrow hole, which looked to be the home of a small animal. She pulled a ripped box over the entrance of the hole, camouflaging herself inside. Sonih overheard the loud arguments on the streets of local townsmen as they resisted the evasion of their homes by militia.

At the same time, across town, the mission where Sonih had hidden was being forcefully ransacked at the lead of her brother, Thamus. Thamus and his men showed no mercy as the trashed the mission, leaving it in disarray. Thamus walked close to the chaplain—his eyes showed a dominance and detachment that fearfully overwhelmed the chaplain. As Thamus's stance settled, the two men stood nose-to-nose, and the tall chaplain felt as if he were in the presence of evil.

"Have you seen my sister?" the young man flatly inquired. "She was kidnapped yesterday, and we are so excited to find her," Thamus explained.

The chaplain spoke softly, trying to seem sincere, "I am so sorry to hear that. I am sorry, but I have not seen her in several months."

Thamus smiled and turned his back to the chaplain. When he spun back around, he held a handgun tight to the chaplain's forehead. The chaplain began to sweat as Thamus forced the chaplain against the wall.

Thamus's tone deepened as he clarified his demands, "I was not asking you. You tell me where my sister is!"

The chaplain closed his eyes, and his airway tightened with panic.

"OK," Thamus replied, just prior to the penetrating discharge of his firearm.

The chaplain's body toppled forward, falling facedown on the brick floor. Thamus looked one of the chaplain's coworkers in the eyes and puckered his lips up, making a mocking kissy face, as she desperately tried to aid the fallen chaplain. Thamus turned a walked away; he and his subordinate soldiers erupted with laughter as the left the mission.

STOLEN AWAY

The day after arriving in Sakakah, the Jacobs family decided that for safety reason, Alan would go alone to the site that had been the target of so much of Jenna's obsession. This was the day after the raid on Sakakah. Alan and Jenna woke early to the sound of weeping in the streets. They peered from the clouded window of their motel to see a horizon of destruction. Alan dressed quickly, wanting to keep their visit as brief as possible. Alan sat on the bed next to his wife and held her hand softly. He pleaded with her to stay in the motel until he came back. Jenna nodded somberly in agreement.

"I love you forever," Alan spoke with a deep, timeless affection.

"I know," Jenna replied, not liking the tone of her husband's goodbye. It scared her. "I love you, Alan. Forever," she requited as she nestled her face into his neck and gently held the back of his head, letting his thick hair push between her fingers. With eyes closed, they kissed as if it was the first and last time. He stood and walked to the door.

He turned back to her and spoke in nonnegotiable terms. "It's six now, our time. Our flight leaves this afternoon at one in the afternoon. Jenna, if I'm not back by noon, take Thomas and go the airport. No matter what, Jenna, do not miss that flight," Alan demanded as he opened the door and walked out.

"Alan!" Jenna called, still sitting nervously on the bed.

He looked back over his shoulder at her.

"Just come back to me," Jenna pleaded.

He nodded his head acceptingly and quickly started off.

The unfamiliar terrain and hot desert air made the trip slow and monotonous. The map Jenna had given him clearly plotted out the route, but the inconsistencies of the actual town was disorientating. It was nearly nine o' clock by the time he arrived at the location. Its unremarkable appearance allowed it to blend in with surrounds. As Alan walked up to the broken building, he immediately noticed a foul smell that was strong enough to bring him to his knees. He tried to fight his senses, but his stomach began cramping repeatedly forward with dry heaves until he finally vomited. Feeling slightly relieved, he rose to his feet. He covered the cloth from his head wrap tightly across his nose and mouth, hoping to minimize the offensive odors. He grabbed the remains of a broken board and started into the building. He used the broken piece of wood to move the trash around and tapped along the interior walls, hoping to find something extraordinary within its charred remains. When the search inside was unsuccessful, he walked along the outside borders. Two dogs that were rummaging through the trash outside broke into an aggressive fight over the rotting corpse of a rabbit. Alan swung violently at the animals with his board and yelled, until he scared them off. Alan was beginning to feel light-headed and thirsty but pushed on through the physical and mental exhaustion. He kicked through the trash, keeping an open mind to the possibilities of what he might be looking for. Suddenly, his leg slid through a wet cardboard box and into a shallow hole, where he was startled by a woman's moan. In surprise, he dropped to his knees and started digging in the filthy sand with his hands.

"Come out!" he demanded.

Hearing the deep American voice, she ventured out in a vulnerable curiosity. She stood proudly, but her petite frame was still shadowed by his overwhelmingly large, broad, solid frame. Though his size might have been intimidating to many natives, she saw only kindness in his face.

"Help me," Sonih spoke with pleading eyes.

The hair on his arm stood straight, and though his skin was pinked with sunburn, chills ran through him. Alan was dazed by the unbelievable events that had led him to this place, this time.

"Hurry, come with me," Alan coaxed.

They ran in unison, and he worked to shield her from onlookers as they rushed back to the motel. It was almost twelve by the time Alan and Sonih retreated back to meet Jenna and Thomas.

Alan interrupted the distressing silence of the void motel when he knocked abruptly on the wooden door. Jenna jumped to her feet and veered through the peephole to find Alan on the other side of the door. She flung open the door with penetrating tears of rejoice and grabbed Alan, pulling him inside the room. Her sobbing was uninterrupted by Alan's gentle reassurances. Jenna just pushed her face into his chest and clung around his waist with a surprising strength.

"Jenna, this is Sonih," Alan stated.

She did not recognize his words.

"Jenna," Alan repeated. "This is Sonih," Alan emphasized.

Jenna looked up and was frozen with incomprehension.

"Sonih?" she mumbled back to him in questioning.

"She's in trouble, Jenna. She needs us to take her away from here," Alan informed.

Jenna was dumbfounded but nodded in a passive agreement.

"I just don't know how were going to get her on that flight. We only have three tickets, and her face is very well known around here," Alan reasoned.

"I know," Jenna agreed. "A solider came by earlier, showed me her picture, and searched the hotel room," she continued.

"They'd never let her on that flight," Alan consulted.

Jenna paused in mental absorption of their present dilemma. Jenna's eyes scanned the room, searching for ideas, and settled on Thomas.

"His wheelchair," Jenna suggested. "Sonih is so petite. She could curl up in the back of the wheelchair, and Thomas could sit on her, and we could cover them with a blanket or something."

"Or we could put them both in sweat pants and a baggy T-shirt," Alan added.

"But the flight is so long," Jenna remembered. "How could she possibly be still for that long and not make a sound?" Jenna inquired.

"A tonic," Sonih presented. "Dealers around the city sell lots of drugs, some make people nearly comatose for hours until they wake up."

Alan and Jenna looked at each other fearfully.

"I don't see any other solutions. Do you?" Alan asked.

"No, I don't. This just might work," Jenna spoke hopefully.

Quickly, Alan hugged Thomas tightly, lifting him up to a nearly standing position. Sonih stood on the wheelchair and stepped carefully into the back of Thomas's sweatpants, making sure her feet went down as far as possible without exiting the pants. She repeated the process with the long-sleeved T-shirt; both were baggy and loose in appearance. Jenna helped them both to a sitting position as Alan lowered them back into the bulky wheelchair. Jenna ensured Sonih was OK. She pushed them in the wheelchair through security and awaited Alan at the terminal. Alan went ahead to find "the tonic." Alan arrived only minutes later at the terminal, finding little resistance in acquiring drugs locally.

He leaned down and hugged Thomas and kissed his cheek, whispering to Sonih, "I found the tonic, with this dose you'll sleep for twenty-four hours."

Alan held the vial to the back of Thomas's neck, and he felt a delicate hand pull it out of his grasp. Alan was still crouching down and talking to Thomas when he noticed the empty vial reappear at the back of Thomas's neck. Alan quickly retrieved the empty vial and slid it into his pocket. They boarded the plane ten minutes later without complications.

BREAKOUT

Hellbound and the remaining volunteers arrived back in Sakakah. Will wove through the intercity with the exhausted jeep. He arrived back at the mission and in one solid movement leaped from the driver's seat and sprinted into the building. He felt shooting pains penetrate his chest as he discovered all the destruction. Hellbound stepped over sprays of blood, and he prepared his mind for the worst. When he spotted the ministers slumped forward on the hard, wooded ground, he ran to him, knelt beside him, and tried to turn him over. His skin was already cool to the touch, and his body was stiffened. Hellbound jumped back to his feet and franticly searched the rest of the small building. He heard movements behind the room at the end of the hall and swung the door open. He found the two female assistants huddled in the corner clinging to each other and whimpering. Hellbound demanded the whereabouts of Sonih to the frazzled women. To Hellbound's frustration, they failed to recognize his words and were of no help. Hellbound reassembled his phone and reconnected with Will in order to update him on their current location and the status of the volunteers. Hellbound was advised to stay inside the mission with the volunteers and a German rescue flight would arrive as soon as possible. For once, Hellbound did as instructed. He brought the shaken volunteers into the ransacked mission and waited—just waited. Now it was only time that tormented him, interrupted periodically by thoughts of regret and worry for

Sonih. It was after midnight by the time the German rescue flight landed and secured the mission. Hellbound and the rest of the volunteers boarded the helicopter and ascended promptly back home, back to Germany.

2019.11.28

THANKSGIVING

Alan, Jenna, and Thomas arrived at the Toledo after midnight. Sonih had kept perfectly hidden within Thomas's baggy attire, the wheelchair, and blankets. Jenna checked Sonih a last time to ensure regular respirations. Alan eagerly pushed Thomas off the airplane, and Jenna followed. Jenna and Alan rushed to the parking lot, leaving their bags unclaimed.

Philip, a close friend of the Jacobs, was waiting in running vehicle in the pickup zone. Alan pulled the door open and lifted his young son with ease into the back seat. Jenna jumped into the middle seat beside Thomas, and together, Alan and Jenna carefully transferred Sonih's flaccid body into the back seat. Alan was still panting with fear when he settled into the front passenger seat. Jenna fought to arouse the sedated youth, but they didn't see any movement outside of her respirations. Sonih made no attempts to open her eyes or speak. She remained deeply in a peaceful coma. They focused on the easy, regular breaths and the rhythmic breathing movements seen in the child's chest.

"When will she wake?" Jenna clarified, already knowing Alan's answer.

"The man said she'd sleep for a whole day. Twenty-four hours," Alan spoke bluntly.

"Minus the twelve-hour flight and travel time," Jenna reminded him.

"She should be awake by morning," Alan decided, and the couple both nodded in agreement.

Later they hovered around the bed of the sleeping child, drifting in and out of sleep themselves, but the child never roused. She just lay limp in the bed, with no subtle shifts or twitches, as seen normally with sleep. It was an unnatural, lingering sleep. Morning came, then evening, and then morning again, but there was no change in Sonih's condition. Jenna and Alan cradled a cup of coffee in the morning, deliberating their next move when they heard a high-pitched musical shrill come from the bedroom. They ran to find Sonih's breathing had changed now. The child now was irregularly gasping for air and shifting periodically to rapid shallow movements, which appeared ineffective. Jenna held the child, and Alan ran to the phone and called 911.

"Help. She's dying. Hurry!" Alan screamed panic-stricken at the emergency attendant.

2019.12.1

LOST AT HOME

Hellbound was reunited with Will in Germany. Will recognized immediately that this was not the same young man he'd known only weeks earlier. They hugged like brothers, grabbed a twelve-pack of Coronas, and talked for hours. Although there were few details Hellbound left out, his story was void of emotion, and he made no mention of Sonih. They both went to bed, but Hellbound found no rest. He lingered in thought, getting up several times that night to vomit.

Over the next few months, Hellbound lost himself in school, work, and a mixed martial arts gym he began attending as a distraction from his racing mind. He always carried a deep and sobering look. He felt restless and lost, but it was his insatiable fury and unrelenting determination that moved him quickly up the ranks at his mixed martial arts gym. The teacher was a Brit named Austin, who saw great potential in Hellbound and soon asked him to travel with the team and enter MMA tournaments around Germany.

BREAK POINT

Sonih was now on life support at the critical care unit at a nearby hospital. Her head was cocked awkwardly toward the ceiling, and a plastic tube descended into her throat, harnessed into her mouth like a horse. She was entangled under tubes from the ventilator, multiple IVs, and a urinary catheter. The Jacobs were allowed in the room now that the medical team deemed her "serious but stable." They nervously awaited the doctor's prognosis. They turned when they heard a knock on the door. A short, stout man with a full gray beard entered the room.

"I'm Dr. Temen," the man announced as he offered his hand to Alan.

Alan quickly returned the handshake.

"What did you find out, Doctor?" Jenna demanded nervously.

The doctor took a deep breath and delivered his prognosis as if it was a prewritten speech. His tone was generic and monotonous.

"Mr. and Mrs. Jacobs, the girl has developed a pulmonary embolism. She has also shown evidence of a stroke. We're not sure yet how much of her brain has been affected."

"How?" Jenna muttered.

"She was at increased clotting risk due to several factors, immobility being one factor," the doctor continued, clearing his throat before going on. "She was also found to have a large amount of GBH in her system," Dr. Temen announced.

The Jacobs looked confused.

"The date rape drug," Dr. Temen clarified bluntly. "Also, pregnancy naturally increases the risk for clots," Dr. Temen informed.

"What?" Jenna insisted. "She's pregnant?" Alan questioned.

"Yes," Dr. Temen responded, and his tone changed quickly, and he coldly added, "There are some people here to see you," the doctor informed flatly, and with that, Dr. Temin nodded at the Jacobs, turned his back to them, and excused himself from the room. Another man walked in. He was thin, tall, and wore a dirty blond, neatly trimmed beard and mustache. He had a pastel-blue polo shirt tucked tightly into his cache slacks.

"I'm Brenten McAnthony. I'm a social worker with the state. I just have a few questions for you both."

He informed calmly while warmly smiling with reassurance. Jenna reached for Alan's hand, and he pulled her close to him.

"How did you come to find this child?" Brenten asked curiously.

"I can't answer that," Alan responded.

The social worker raised his eyebrows with surprise and continued on, "Well, maybe you could tell me how this child consumed a toxic amount of the date rate drug or how a child seemingly under seventeen years old and newly pregnant?" Brenten asked accusingly.

Alan and Jenna were frozen and speechless.

"I didn't know she was pregnant," Jenna's voice cracked with emotion and eyes welled up with tears.

"Just pregnant," Mr. McAnthony continued. "Due date was estimated by a blood test. If the story you gave the doctors upon admission is legitimate, that leaves the sole responsibility on you, Mr. Jacobs," Brenten concluded.

With that statement, two armed state troopers marched into the room and began reciting the Miranda rights to Mr. Jacobs after notifying him he was under arrest for the kidnapping, assault, and sexual abuse of a youth. Jenna weakly forced out pleas of her husband's innocence behind a flood of tears. The officers cuffed Alan and escorted him out of the room. Jenna dropped to her knees, sobbing and speechless. Thomas was quietly unaware of the intruders.

"Jenna, just take care of Thomas and the girl. Don't worry about me. I'll be fine, Jenna," Alan reassured.

The months to follow were like a nightmare for Jenna. She spent the days in the hospital with Sonih and had nightly meetings with the defense attorney regarding Alan's charges. He was still in jail. There was no allowable bond related to severity of the charges. The few occasions Jenna had been allowed visit Alan had been devastating. At each visit, Alan looked freshly beaten with an assortment of bruises and cuts along with a reddened and swollen face. Each time she questioned what happened, and each time Alan smiled and said, "Nobody likes a child abuser."

Before she could break with tears, Alan comforted her. "This world must not be as far gone as it seems sometimes. This is how a child abuser deserves to be treated," Alan reasoned.

"You're not a rapist" Jenna countered emotionally.

"They don't know that," Alan said with a smile and hugged Jenna passionately.

The trial was scheduled to begin in three months. The prosecution requested an extension due to the complexity and sensitivity of the case, and it was granted. Alan wouldn't defend himself. He didn't attempt to create an elaborate story or indulge the attorneys with the truth.

Back at the hospital, Sonih's condition continued to be "stable yet serious"—laymen's terms, she was still in a coma with irreversible brain damage. The only noted movements was the mechanical rise and fall in Sonih's chest along with the gentle kicks that now jerked her distended abdomen. Jenna could feel the powerful presence of the baby long before he arrived. Jenna would spend hours with her hands cupped around Sonih's growing abdomen, feeling the movements and shifts of the unborn child.

2020.5.31

FINDING THE SON(IH)

Hellbound found great success in his tournaments around Germany, beating his opponents with boundless determination. He also joined Austin in a tournament in London, England. The English competitors were more experienced, but Hellbound flourished, winning both his matches by decision. He stayed with Austin and his family for a month, in London.

From there, they traveled to a subsequent tournament in Detroit, Michigan. Hellbound won his match in Detroit with a knockout in the third round. Hellbound had experienced travels and victory he'd never dreamt of, but he found no peace in it. He was still lost and restless. He found no sleep in the quiet of night, only absence of distractions from his own racing mind. Hellbound easily maintained his middle-weight requirements, as results of the frequent vomiting that still plagued him, due to climaxed worries over Sonih. Hellbound was packing his suitcase, preparing for their return flight, when he got an overwhelming feeling he should turn on the TV.

He sat on the end of the bed, watching the news, and he became overcome with severe nausea and ran to the bathroom to vomit.

"You throw up a lot, Jackson, are you sick or something?" Austin questioned concernedly.

Hellbound just held up his hand toward Austin, requesting silence, watching the news intently, and added, "Don't call me Jackson."

The news was covering the trial of a man accused of kidnapping along with criminal sexual assault of a minor. They told of the victim, a pregnant teen, who remained in a coma in a Toledo hospital. They were unable to identify the name or origin, of the minor, but named the accused man as Alan Jacobs of Dayton, Ohio. They showed pictures of the youth and pleaded for anyone who has any information on the name of this youth to please contact the Toledo, Ohio, Police Department.

"That's Sonih!" Hellbound screamed with mixed emotions of both relief and fear.

Hellbound felt feverish and nervous. He began sweating profusely. He felt his chest tighten as he struggled to breath.

"What? Who's Sonih?" Austin questioned with a deeply perplexed look on his face.

"My wife," Hellbound demanded.

"What the fuck is the matter with you?" Austin inquired, becoming increasingly alarmed by Hellbound's bizarre behaviors.

Austin suggested something trying to defuse the situation. "Let's just get out of here. We've got a plane to catch," Austin urged, trying to defuse the situation. "We've got a plane to catch, buddy," Austin emphasized.

"No! I got to get Sonih!" Hellbound was emotionally beyond reasoning. "I'm not getting on that flight," Hellbound spoke challengingly.

Austin walked calmly in front of the door.

"I don't know what's going on with you, man. You don't have a wife, and you don't know that girl on the TV. You're not going anywhere unless it's on a flight home," Austin demanded, now changing his tone to one of stern dominance.

"Are you going to stop me?" Hellbound questioned while smiling an ironic display of conquest.

"I've got a few pounds on you, boss, let's not let it go too far," Austin pleaded.

Hellbound just stood smiling arrogantly at Austin.

"I know that trip was intense and you've had a lot of challenges in your life, kid. I'm going to call Will, buddy. He can help us sort this all out," Austin reasoned.

"You do that while I go take a walk to unwind," Hellbound spoke sarcastically.

"Just a second, and I'll go with you," Austin insisted.

"Hey, Will, it's Austin. Jackson kind of snapped here. He's not acting right, and he's not making any sense," Austin spoke into the receiver. "He's talking about going to get his wife, some girl in a coma on the TV over here. I don't know what he's going to try to do."

Just then, Hellbound darted toward the door. Austin leaped toward him, dropping the receiver on the bed. Hellbound swung around with a right hook to Austin's jaw. Austin pushed through the punch, tackling Hellbound against the wall. Austin surged two quick right knees into Hellbound's gut as Hellbound struggled to his feet, pinched tightly against the wall. Hellbound jumped up on Austin, locking his head up, and pushed away from the wall, with the force of both legs. The two fell forward with Hellbound in the mounted position, and Austin wrapped up Hellbound's arms. Hellbound offended with a determined head bunt to the bridge of Austin's nose. Hellbound jumped to his feet and escaped out the door, quickly grabbing the keys to the rental car. Austin sprung to his feet, with blood now heavily flowing out of his nose, saturating the front of his shirt. Austin tightly pinched the bridge of his nose and held the wadded shirt to his face as a barrier against the blood. Scared guests cleared the halls as Hellbound raced by. Hellbound stopped momentarily.

"It's just something I have to do," he urged as he looked sincerely at Austin.

"Do you know how weird you are?" Austin said, shaking his head in unbelief.

The two friends shook hands, smiled, and then Hellbound proceeded out the front doors of the hotel.

I don't know how I'm going to explain this mess to Will, Austin mumbled to himself.

CRASH

Jenna and Thomas sat alongside Sonih, and the ultrasound tech came in for a routine fetal check. She gave Jenna a disgusted look, which Jenna was now accustomed to.

"Is there a problem?" Jenna asked, irritated by the tech's rude behavior.

"I just don't think it's appropriate for you to be here, with everything that's going on," the tech voiced as she prepared her equipment.

"She's our friend. It's not like everyone thinks. There's nowhere else we'd be," Jenna rebuked, trying to bite her tongue.

The tech rolled her eyes as she began the fetal check. Within a minute, the mood had changed to one of uncertainty and fear.

"Is everything all right?" Jenna asked, already sensing the answer.

Ultrasounds were done every eight hours routinely, and Jenna had been present on numerous exams, and this time was definitely different.

"The baby's heart rate is low," the ultrasound tech confirmed. "I'll just let the doc know," the tech spoke nervously and weakly faked a smile.

She quickly fled the room, leaving her equipment at the bedside. Jenna cradled Sonih's hand and stroked her hair, nurturing, while repeatedly whispering, "He's going to be OK, pretty girl."

Jenna's words consoled only herself as the unconscious teen lay unaware.

A moment later, a young intruder pushed through the door. Nurses attempted to barricade the entrance, while one nurse yelled, "Call security," back to the nurse's station. Hellbound froze in unbelief. His eyes welled with tears, and he dropped to his knees.

"Can I help you?" Jenna asked cautiously as he approached the visibly tormented youth.

His voice wavered with emotion. "This is my wife," Hellbound voiced aloud in disbelief.

A baffled look spread across the room, and everyone stopped speechless. Then the nurses attempted to escort the young man back into the hall.

"STOP!" Jenna yelled. "Leave us," Jenna demanded.

The nurses turned to Jenna. "Ma'am, you really don't have the authority," a nurse voiced snobbishly.

Jenna interrupted the bias staff. Jenna looked directly into their eyes and spoke with an uncharacteristic vengeance.

"You have been unbelievably rude throughout this whole hospitalization. I am the only friend she has right now. The state-appointed guardian has authorized me to be here. The police clearly don't have any suspicion that I did anything wrong, or I would be locked up with my husband already. He stays with me!" Jenna yelled erratically back at the nurses.

With her comment, the nurses released Hellbound's arms and abruptly left the room with a sighs of anger.

The troubled teen still on his knees struggled to catch his breath. Jenna helped him to his feet. He was immediately drawn to Sonih. He gently held her face and softly pressed his cheek to hers.

"I don't understand, how?" Hellbound struggled to complete his sentence. "How? What happened to her?" Hellbound sorrowfully rambled.

He looked to Jenna for answers as he rubbed the tears from his reddened eyes.

"What's her name?" Jenna inquired of him. "I haven't even told the staff her true name," Jenna informed him.

Hellbound looked to Jenna. "This is Sonih," he said with certainty.

"Yes, it is!" Jenna said with an elated smile. "She wanted us to sneak her out of the country. She took some tonic from a street dealer to make her sleep and keep hidden during the return flight. The doctors said she threw blood clots that went to her lungs and brain. They had to vent her to keep her alive, to keep the baby alive," Jenna emphasized. "I'm so sorry, but they've said she's brain-dead, and now the tech just said baby he may be in danger. They're notifying the doctor now," Jenna vented to the young man, feeling a weight lift from her shoulders.

Hellbound looked confused as he carefully touched Sonih's protruding abdomen. He leaned down and kissed her stomach. He stood back up and looked to Jenna.

"I don't know what to say," Hellbound confessed.

She shook off his statement, and they just smiled to each other.

Suddenly, a flood of medical staff burst into the room with a stretcher in tow.

"The doctor wants to take the baby. He's in crisis," the nurse informed professionally. "You'll want to wear these in surgery," the nurse ordered, holding a folded pair of surgical scrubs outreached.

Jenna retrieved the scrubs and turned to assist Hellbound into the scrubs, while the medical team transferred Sonih onto the stretcher.

"What's your name?" Jenna asked.

"Jackson, but people call me Hellbound," Hellbound responded, and Jenna laughed.

"People aren't always right," Jenna rebuked with a smile.

Hellbound smiled back to her and mouthed, "Thank you," as he followed the stretcher out of the room.

REALIZATION

The surgery went fast, with each team member busily doing their jobs with the precision of bees constructing a hive. The doctor cut an emergency incision, which descended vertically from mid abdomen to Sonih's pubic area. The doctor subsequently cut through deeper layers of tissue until penetrating the uterus. He gave an order to "open," and nurses each aside of Sonih aided in widening the incision. The doctor quickly retrieved the

tiny, motionless baby. The doctor then clamped the cord, cut it, and handed the purple neonate to the awaiting neonate intensive care team. The nurses rubbed the baby and flicked the newborn's feet. To a much-anticipated relief, the infant began crying, and a joyous laughter filled the room.

Hellbound clung to the newborn, cradling the infant within his strong and gentle guard. He soon had to relinquish the premature baby back to the care of the neonate intensive care unit. He wouldn't leave Sonih's side.

He kissed her cheek and whispered softly to her, "I love you, Sonih. Come back to me, Sonih," while the doctor closed the incision.

Later that afternoon, Sonih did slowly begin to come back to him. She opened her eyes briefly for the first time in over six months; this was a feat the doctors assured Jenna would never again happen. The next morning, Sonih was taking occasional breaths on her own, resisting the efforts of the vent. During the course of the next several weeks, she came off the vent and began talking and even eating on her own. The doctors were all baffled by her recovery. The nurses loomed about the room with awestruck expressions. A few reporters even began prodding around the area—until they were discovered and subsequently eradicated by protective medical staff, Jenna, or Hellbound.

The baby was growing beautifully and eating well. They neonatologist didn't expect any long-term residual from the baby's early appearance. One month postpartum, Sonih walked with Hellbound to see their son. The tiny baby lay sleeping within the security of the incubator. Sonih smiled to capacity. Hellbound held Sonih lovingly.

"So what's his name?" Hellbound asked.

Sonih smiled at Hellbound and began speaking about a dream she'd had in the coma, with "an unusual vividness like life," Sonih emphasized.

"He was a powerful baby," she explained. Sonih laughed happily, remembering the dream. "They called him Leium," she recalled.

"Who did?" Hellbound asked.

"The angels in my dream," she said, smiling back at him.

"Leium, it is," Hellbound agreed. "Leium Dai, after your mom," Hellbound suggested with sorrowful eyes that conveyed the loss that he was compelled to tell her about only days earlier.

Sonih nodded approvingly at Hellbound, as gentle tears trickled down her cheeks.

"Leium Dai Herrington," Sonih whispered back to herself, looking at the fragile infant.

CUSTODY

"Where did you come from?" Brenten, the social worker, prodded at Sonih as she lay peacefully in her hospital bed.

"I won't tell you, and I am not going back. It's unsafe," Sonih demanded, making soft eye contact with Brenten.

"I've got a man sitting in jail because of your stubbornness and another young man claiming to be your husband. He just turned eighteen a few weeks ago, and there is no such marriage license on file. And you, young lady, do not look to be of a consenting age," Brenten fumbled aloud through the inconsistencies of this case.

"I'm eighteen. Alan never harmed me. Please let him go. He is a very kind man, and it's deeply saddening to know he's in jail because of me," Sonih pleaded.

Sonih kept powerful eye contact with Brenten as she rebutted his accusations.

"I've got no record of your existence in the US, but here you are. Tell me where you came from, you certainly seem to be foreign," Brenten insinuated of the youth.

Sonih sat speechless but kept steady eye contact with Brenten.

"Just tell me your name," Brenten urged.

"You can call me Ghost, because that's what I am to you," Sonih rebutted.

"Miss, I am on your side, but I' m going to take that baby into protective services if I don't getting answers," Brenten threatened, as his face turned red with frustration.

Sonih smiled softly at Brenten's unfounded threat.

"I would be curious to find a man brave enough to try to take that baby away from his daddy," Sonih jested as she laughed aloud.

She turned toward Hellbound, who was gently cradling the sleeping infant in the corner of her hospital room. Hellbound looked at Sonih and smiled sincerely back at her.

"Mr. Brenten, if you want to see my home, it's right there," Sonih spoke.

Her words were serious and strong as she pointed to Hellbound and the baby.

"Brenten, I can tell you're a good man and are genuinely concerned about my well-being. I am happy and safe now. I don't care what's on paper, this is my husband. Alan is a friend, and I want him out of jail immediately," Sonih pleaded with Brenten.

Brenten smiled at Sonih. "OK, you win," Brenten surrendered.

He sighed as he fumbled through paper, requesting signatures from both Sonih and Hellbound.

Hellbound would be legally responsible for Sonih, along with baby Leium, until Sonih's age could be determined. It was explained that until citizenship papers were returned, reviewed, and approved, Sonih must remain in Ohio. She and Hellbound would also be required to check in weekly with Brenten to ensure safety. Sonih and Hellbound smiled excitedly back at Brenten.

HOMECOMING

"Doctor said you can both go today, right?" Hellbound confirmed with Sonih.

She nodded eagerly, springing up out of the bed and wrapping her arms around him. She just held him, still in unbelief. She savored his smell and the feel of his skin as she nestled her face into his neck. Hellbound picked her up easily and danced her around the room playfully.

"I got some things for the baby last night," Hellbound proudly informed Sonih and then continued. "Jenna said we can stay with her until we find a place. I still have ten thousand in winnings from the tournaments. That will be enough for a down payment on a house and a used car," Hellbound rambled anxiously, but Sonih just smiled at him proudly.

Hellbound, Sonih, and the baby arrived at the Jacobs' modest suburban home. Jenna had set up the basement as a cozy loft. She toured the young family through the house, trying to make them feel welcome. She urged them to relax until she had finished dinner. An hour later, they were gathered around the table for dinner. Jenna smiled at the couple and encouraged them to eat, but Jenna became choked up and excused herself from the table. Sonih quickly stood up and followed Jenna to the living room, where Jenna was hunched over, sobbing uncontrollably into the arm of the sofa. Sonih warmly put her arm over Jenna shoulder and laid her head on Jenna's back.

"Alan is going to get out soon. Brenten assured me he was going today to talk with the prosecutor," Sonih ensured Jenna.

Her words were of little comfort to Jenna, but Jenna sat upright, looked at Sonih, and nodded strongly behind reddened and wet eyes. They hugged, and Jenna sighed deeply, trying to mentally expel her fears and worries. Jenna let out a quiet, embarrassed laugh and coaxed Sonih back to the dinner table.

They boisterously cackled throughout the meal, talking late into the night about the unbelievable trials they had all been through. Jenna felt the weight of the burdens and anger ease as she talked. Jenna felt guilty for enjoying the dinner, knowing Alan probably ate a dry bologna sandwich, in a cold jail cell, while trying to anticipate his next attack from cellmates. They noticed Jenna frequently gazed at her wedding ring throughout the night. Jenna would kiss the ring with closed eyes and forced a subtle broken smile behind an anguished grimace of pain. Sonih excused herself to nurse the baby, in the private comfort of the temporary basement loft. Hellbound followed Sonih after he sincerely hugged Jenna, kissed her check, and whispered, "Thank you."

Sonih nestled into the corner of the couch and nursed Leium. Hellbound sat against the arm of the opposite end of the couch, facing toward Sonih. He pulled his cell phone from his pocket and dialed Will as his did nearly every night. Hellbound laughed as he chatted on the phone for about ten minutes but couldn't help but stare at Sonih and the baby the whole time, overwhelmed by a feeling of amazement.

After the baby was fed, the couple snuggled together, watched TV, and talked over the next day's plans. Jenna tapped modestly on the door and slowly stepped down the stairway. Jenna smiled warmly at the couple, explaining that she couldn't sleep. It was already two in the morning, and the house was still wound up from the busy day. Jenna noticed the baby's eyes open, and Leium looked toward her. Jenna melted by the sight of the beautiful new baby and asked if she could hold him.

Sonih replied, "Of course," and gently placed the infant into Jenna's arms.

"I was just about to get Thomas around for bed. Do you mind if I let him say good night to Leium?" Jenna asked.

"Sure," Hellbound replied as he snuggled in with Sonih.

Jenna overheard the couple's loving talk and giggles as she walked back up the stairs, and it made her long for Alan even more.

Hellbound and Sonih enjoyed solitude for the first time since their reunion. Sonih ran her hand over Hellbound's chest.

"You're so big now," Sonih commented, remembering the less-bulky Hellbound when they first met.

Hellbound still smiled at Sonih. "I can't stop looking at you," he confessed. "I can't believe you're real. It's like I'm in a wonderful dream. I was sick with worry and guilt," he continued. "I left you there." Hellbound's voice choked up as he tried to hide his tears and reddened eyes by lowering his face into his cupped hands. "I thought you were dead. I left you. I'm so sorry," he apologized as he was hunched forward weakly with his heavy, wet, and grimaced face hung toward the ground in shame. He sobbed for the first time in his life. He was too riddled with regret to even consider how weak and vulnerable he was to Sonih.

He felt her warm hand run through his hair, and his face tingled as her hand came to a stop, resting against his cheek. She pulled his face up to her and away from the ground. His eyes still looked toward the floor, resisting her efforts to comfort him. He finally succumbed to her gentle patience and met her eyes with his own. His rugged face recovered momentarily, fighting an instinctive urge to look away. His eyes were deep and true.

"I'm so sorry, Sonih," Hellbound pleaded for forgiveness.

Sonih smiled at him proudly, caught off guard by his confessions. "Hellbound," Sonih called to him lovingly. "You have nothing to be sorry about. I am so proud of you. You saved those people," she voiced as she paused briefly and her stare was frozen to his. "And you saved me," Sonih emphasized.

"Some died. Your mom," Hellbound started.

"Her choice," Sonih interrupted. "She died doing what is right. Don't take that away from her," Sonih cried, and Hellbound nodded to her with understanding.

Then she continued her thoughts aloud. "You, Hellbound, are the only thing I am certain about. I have an overwhelming feeling that you and Leium are my reason, my purpose," She confessed to him as her own eyes began to squint against a flood of emotions. The two smiled at each other and laughed as they melted together.

"I'm so proud to be with you," Hellbound whispered as he leaned to kiss Sonih.

He moistened his lips with his tongue just before their lips pushed together. He felt her spirit and desired for her. Knowing her body was still too fragile from the surgery, he fought against his temptations.

Suddenly, a long shrill scream from upstairs forced them apart, as terror brought them immediately to their feet. The couple sprinted up the stairs with dozens of perceived threats racing through their minds. When they reached the landing, their hearts dropped as they struggled to reorient themselves. Jenna stood pale and speechless, with her mouth hung open. Jenna was panting, and high-pitched wheezes pulled against the force of her tightened chest. The infant was sleeping sound within Jenna's grasp. Sonih quickly retrieved the baby from Jenna.

"What?" Hellbound yelled in panic.

Jenna's body was frozen as her arm stretched outward, pointing toward the living room.

"Thomas," Jenna forced out a weak, whispered voice.

Hellbound and Sonih swung their heads around just as Thomas walked through the room's arched threshold. Sonih gasped in unbelief, and her legs weakened, bringing her to her knees, while still cradling Leium in her arms. Hellbound walked to him in awe, circling the child with examining eyes.

"How! What!" Hellbound rambled anxiously, trying to adapt to his new, distorted reality. "How!" Hellbound repeated.

Jenna was still partially frozen in a distant stare as she started mumbling softly.

"I was helping Thomas to hold the baby. He was still in his wheelchair. We were holding the baby. Thomas started making noise and jerking around. I grabbed the baby up. I thought Thomas must be having a seizure. Then he stood up. Thomas just stood right up out of his wheelchair." Jenna shook her head in disbelief of her own words.

Jenna slowly stepped toward her son. She was filled with fear.

"Thomas?" Jenna called to him. "Sweetheart, is this really happening?" Jenna cried.

Thomas stood proudly with a glowing smile. His face was handsome and strong; his body was no longer twisted by awkward muscle movement and contractures.

"Mom, it's me," Thomas spoke with perfect articulation as if he'd been speaking all along. "Believe it, Mom," Thomas tried to reassure Jenna.

Jenna grabbed the child into a careful hug. She was still partially disorientated by recent events.

"How?" Jenna cried as joyful tears silhouetted her cheeks.

Thomas lovingly smiled at his mom as he pulled from her grasp and walked to Sonih. She was seated on her heels with knees bent. The child was still secure in her arms. Thomas eased to his knees in front of Sonih, and he leaned forward to kiss the baby.

"Leium," Thomas laughed as he was overfilled with happiness.

Chills ran through the room as everyone turned to stare at the infant. Their expressions were puzzled. Hellbound now settled into a seated position on the floor, with himself, Jenna, and Sonih circled around the room's border. Thomas retreated to the center of the room, testing out his new physical limits. Thomas jumped, spun, and danced around the room. Jenna, Sonih, and Hellbound watched intrigued and laughed proudly at each trick. Thomas raced around the house, up and down the basement stairs, each time reappearing in the living room to receive a much-anticipated applaud from his eager audience. After hours of rediscovering his body, Thomas lay in the middle of the room, sighing with exhaustion.

Thomas turned to Jenna. "I'm tired," he spoke smiling.

Jenna giggled and crawled over to the child. She seated herself Indian-style next to him and began stroking his forehead and hair as she had done to induce sleep thousands of times before. Jenna beamed with pride and amazement at her son. It was now five thirty in the morning, and Thomas and Leium were the only two that had found sleep. The others buzzed around the house, eating and preparing for the day.

JAIL BREAK

"Alan comes home today," Hellbound cheered optimistically.

Jenna smiled at him and nodded. "Yes," Jenna said as she danced around the kitchen.

Hellbound and Jenna left the house at seven thirty, making sure they were at the jailhouse before the business office opened at eight. They stood anxiously on the outside of the tellers' podiums. The metal curtain rolled upward, exposing a uniformed officer behind the glass divider.

"We're here for Alan Jacobs," Jenna spoke quickly to the officer. "His charges were dropped this morning," Jenna continued.

The heavy officer, who tested the limits of his uniform, fumbled through paperwork and computer screens, trying to validate Jenna's information.

The officer cleared his throat before speaking. "I'm sorry, ma'am. I don't have the details yet, but I can call you when I clarify things."

As the officer spoke, his thick, gray mustache prodded against his lower lip.

"Get on the phone, sir. This needs to be clarified now. I have no intentions on leaving without Alan," Jenna demanded of the officer.

The officer looked offended but retreated, back to a desk as he rolled his eyes, annoyed with Jenna's statement. Jenna and Hellbound stood watching him as he grabbed on the phone for about ten minutes. Finally, he got up and moved back up to the information desk.

"OK, ma'am. I've got it confirmed. It will just be a few minutes to get him processed out of the system," the officer updated.

With completion of his statement, the officer smiled at Jenna. Jenna grabbed Hellbound, and they jumped up and down, overjoyed by their success.

Jenna and Hellbound paced the waiting area, anxiously awaiting Alan. Six minutes later, a different uniformed officer escorted Alan to the waiting area. Alan was holding a paper bag of belongings. He wore street clothes, multiple stages of bruises, cuts, and a limitless smile. The officer opened the dividing door to reunite Alan with his wife. Alan and Jenna ran to each other and hugged each other tightly. Jenna covered Alan's face with quick, wet kisses.

"Let's go," Alan urged.

With his request, they exited the police station and quickly jumped into the car. It was moments before Alan looked behind him, into the back seat, surprised by Jenna's male companion.

"Who are you?" Alan demanded of the perceived intruder.

"This is Hellbound. He's staying with us," Jenna interrupted.

Alan's eyes turned to Jenna with a confused anger. Jenna laughed, embarrassed by Alan's insinuating expression.

"No. This is Sonih's husband. They're staying with us until they find a house," Jenna clarified.

At the sound of her name, Alan's mind shifted to one of concern. "Is Sonih all right?" Alan questioned nervously.

"She's perfect. She's recovered beyond doctors' expectations," Jenna informed him happily.

"It's a miracle," Alan commented. "They said she was brain-dead. She was on the vent," Alan remembered.

"There's been another miracle, Alan," Jenna beamed, stretching her mouth tightly upward in an enormous smile.

Alan's eyes looked to Jenna, and he cocked his head slightly and tightening his brow in question.

"It's Thomas," she confessed proudly. "He walks and talks. He's perfectly healthy," Jenna finished.

Alan looked at her like she was crazy. "No, Jenna. That's not possible," Alan spoke softly and looked at Jenna with pity.

"I'm not crazy, Alan. You'll see, sweetheart. It's amazing," Jenna beamed.

Upon arriving back home, Alan sprung from the car and sprinted inside the house. Alan scanned the house for his son.

"Thomas," Alan called, searching throughout the house. "Thomas," Alan repeatedly yelled.

A distant, "Dad, I'm outside," echoed from the backyard.

With Thomas's call, Alan spun around to peer through the living room window. Alan's heart jumped in his chest, and his stomach twisted as if he were on a diving roller coaster. Alan's now-shaking and weak legs clumsily fought to run to Thomas. Alan slid open the glass door and sprinted into the yard, where the child was playing. Alan was oblivious to Sonih's presence as he raced past her lying relaxed on a folding cot with newborn snuggled to her chest. Thomas and Alan excitedly narrowed the distance between each other with open sprints. Alan's mind struggled to recognize the child as his son. Upon meeting, Alan grabbed Thomas up into his strong arms, swinging him back and forth like a baby.

"Daddy!" Thomas yelled excitedly. "I missed you, Daddy. I can walk now, Daddy," Thomas bragged as Alan stood speechless, tearfully nodding his head with a proud understanding. "Look what else I can do, Daddy!" Thomas proudly boasted as he wiggled free of his father's hug.

Thomas did a cartwheel, fumbled to his feet, and bounced up and down proudly, smiling up at his father upon completion. Alan laughed with joy.

"What's that called, Daddy?" Thomas inquired.

Before Alan could answer, Thomas continued, "Look how fast I can run, Daddy." Thomas quickly informed before circling the yard in a full sprint.

The child returned to Alan, breathlessly inquiring about how long it took him to sprint the length of the yard. Alan grabbed the child up again in a loving hug.

"I love you, Thomas, and I'm so happy you can run now."

Alan forced out choked a wavering speech. Alan planted several quick kisses on Thomas's face before he wiggled away again to display another accomplishment to his father.

Jenna sat in a folding lounge chair next to Sonih and the baby. Jenna was happily watching the father and son's reunion for over an hour before intruding with a camera like an overbearing Pavarotti. Soon Jenna prepared for a picnic by setting the picnic table with store-bought potato salad, warm hot dogs, baked beans, and lemonade. They gathered around the table, reacquainting Alan with the last several months' trials and blessings. Jenna felt an overwhelming feeling of peace and calm, something uncharacteristic of her restless spirit. Jenna soaked in the warmth of the sun and savored the beauty of the day and the growing family that now surrounded her.

HOUSE HUNTING

The next day, Hellbound and Sonih woke early. They had planned to meet with a local real estate agent who was going to show them some houses in the area. They crept upstairs and found Alan and Jenna sitting side by side at the kitchen table, giggling like teenagers and sipping coffee.

"Good morning," Sonih said while cradling the sleeping infant in her arms.

"Wonderful morning," Alan corrected, smiling at Jenna as he pushed a kiss onto her cheek.

"We were going to set Leium up in the bathroom while we showered, but since you're up, can he sit with you?" Hellbound asked as he cradled an infant, carrying basket under one arm.

"We'd love to," Jenna interjected.

Sonih nestled the baby in the basket, kissed his lips sweetly, and smiled with gratitude at the Jacobs. Sonih was drawn to hug Jenna as she was overcome by all they continued to sacrifice for her.

"Thank you for everything," Sonih said with sincerity as she pulled away from Jenna.

Jenna smiled humbly and said, "It's nothing."

Hellbound easily grabbed Sonih up, nodded at Alan, and proceeded down the hall while Sonih giggled playfully.

"We're going to the shower," Hellbound yelled, momentarily turned back toward Jenna and Alan.

Hellbound pushed the ajar door open with his foot while he playfully nibbled at Sonih's neck, growling softly like a dog. Sonih exploded into uncontrollable laughter as she coyly fought free of his hold. Sonih tried to adjust the temperature on the water despite Hellbound's determination to distract her. Hellbound hugged Sonih from behind, holding her arms securely to her abdomen as he sloppily kissed her ear and nibbled again on her neck. Sonih's laughter erupted again as she tried to refocus Hellbound's efforts.

"We have to meet the real estate agent in an hour," Sonih blurted, fighting against her interruptive laughter.

Hellbound let her go, sat on the edge on the tub, slumped forward, and pouted dramatically with his facial expressions.

"You're not right," Sonih giggled.

Hellbound's expression changed to one of amusement as he gave his best effort at seductive bedroom eyes.

"I'll never be bored, will I?" Sonih laughed.

Hellbound just smiled at her as if she were the northern lights after a season of Alaskan darkness.

Sonih undressed slowly, keeping a constant eye contact on Hellbound. Her expression turned flat, with careful attention to his actions and expressions for interpretation. He was still, and his mouth hung open nervously for moments until he quickly wiped the drool from his lips and closed his mouth with realization of his awkwardness. She turned her back to him and gracefully slid into the steamy shower and was then clouded by the humid fog. He followed her, still fully dressed, before reflexively pulling back from the scorching water. He cautiously held himself against the wall of the shower, fighting temptation to reenter the burning water.

"It's too hot!" Hellbound whined.

"Then get out," Sonih playfully suggested.

Hellbound instead tried to reach around Sonih to adjust the hot water nozzle. She swatted away his attempts as he reactively yelped against the shooting hot sting of the water. He jumped out of the shower, carelessly flooding water on the tile floor.

"It's too hot!" Hellbound demanded, reaching protectively from outside the shower. "How can you even stand it?" he questioned.

"OK, turn it down," Sonih submitted. "But you need to take your clothes off," Sonih negotiated.

Hellbound shot a cocky smile at her and pulled the soaked T-shirt over his head. She was breathlessly in awe of his defined chest and was mesmerized by the way the water trickled down his hard chest.

"I can't believe you're my husband," Sonih spoke humbly.

Hellbound smiled slightly before confidently letting his shirt drop on the wet tile with a splat. He eagerly undressed before silently joining her in the shower. He stood motionless on the edge of the water's stream. She walked toward him with acceptance and pushed herself on tipped toes, forcing a deep kiss onto his lips. He stood desperately savoring the taste of her mouth. He throbbed with longing for her, until he instinctively pulled her to him. Hellbound felt the warmth of her bust push against his chest and the subtle movements of her wet stomach and prickles of the sutures of her incision line against his pelvis. He stepped away from her slowly.

"Remember what the doctor said," Hellbound prompted. "Eight weeks," he reminded.

Sonih smiled lovingly back at him as he ran his hand gently down the series of staples vertically descending from her navel to pelvis. He knelt down and kissed the incision line. A surge of tingles raced through her, and she knelt down with him and held his cheek as they looked at each other adoringly. Hellbound opened the shampoo and squeezed a handful of its contents into his hands. He worked a thick lather into Sonih's long dark hair and meticulously massaged the shampoo throughout her hair and scalp.

"I love you," Hellbound spoke with a penetrating seriousness.

Sonih nodded knowingly. "I love you," she requited.

"I know," he said. "I can feel it," Hellbound added.

Sonih smiled at him as she arched her head backward, closed her eyes, and allowed the water to rinse the suds from her hair. Hellbound intently watched the flood of soap bubbles race down her strong body and collect in a pool at her knees. He didn't speak. He just leaned in with gentle kisses that bordered the nape of her jaw. He expressionlessly soaped a washcloth and gently slid it along every curve on her body. She wanted him, and her eyes naively displayed every emotion like words in a book. She pulled the cloth from his hand and ran it along his neck and trunk, paying careful attention to the muscular cuts in his chest and shoulders. He submissively knelt before her as she firmly scrubbed him, becoming familiar with his entire body. Hellbound was weak with lust for Sonih but fought against temptations, knowing her body was still healing from the coma and the C-section.

They crept from the shower, down the stairs to their temporary basement loft. Upon realizing the time, they hurried to get dressed and collect a few necessities for the baby. They hiked back upstairs, thanked the Jacobs for watching Leium, and carefully tucked the still-sleeping infant into his car seat.

"You said we could take the car, right?" Hellbound clarified.

"Of course," Alan said, nodding happily.

"Good luck," Jenna added.

Hellbound nodded at the Jacobs with appreciation as Sonih gathered some fruit and coffee for the trip. Hellbound and Sonih beamed with anticipation for the day's adventure.

"Sonih," Hellbound said calmly, engaging in serious eye contact with Sonih.

"Who's Leium's dad?" Hellbound spoke flatly, still watching the road while driving.

Sonih was quiet. "You are," she blurted back, assuring him.

"I love him and will raise him as my own, but you and I both know we've not been together. There's no way he's my biological son," Hellbound spoke shortly.

"I don't know. I've not had any man yet," Sonih said. "I woke up from a long coma with a baby. I don't remember anything of a man," Sonih continued. "You believe me, don't you?" Sonih added.

Hellbound dodged the question with a question of his own.

"You don't think Alan?" Hellbound suggested.

"No," Sonih blurted back, interrupting Hellbound's offensive questioning. "I know people. He's a good man," Sonih defended.

"You're naive to how twisted some people can be," Hellbound scolded.

"I assure you, I know firsthand how evil people can be," Sonih spoke firmly. "Anyway, the hospital admission was the day after we landed in Ohio. The test results showed I was one week pregnant," Sonih clarified.

"Then you had a boyfriend at home?" Hellbound suggested.

"No," Sonih snapped back. "No boyfriend! No sex! Nothing!" she clarified shortly.

"We weren't together," Hellbound demanded.

"I know! I was there!" Sonih yelled.

"Don't mess with me, Sonih. Babies don't just appear," Hellbound spoke calmly but seriously. "I don't care about it. I love you. I forgive you," Hellbound prompted.

Sonih sighed, visibly annoyed. "Look at me, Hellbound." Sonih tried to calm herself. "I don't understand it either, but you have to trust me. I won't lie to you. There was no one," Sonih spoke calmly.

"Alan then?" Hellbound muttered. "The lab dates must have been off," Hellbound continued.

"No!" Sonih yelled in opposition.

Hellbound punched the steering wheel with frustration, causing a short blast from the horn.

"Just don't talk about it anymore," Hellbound spoke flatly.

Sonih unbuckled her seat belt and climbed into the back seat, turning her back to him with annoyance.

"Are you blind, Hellbound? To everything that has happened? To Leium? Miracles? My dreams," Sonih spoke with a deepening brow. "This is bigger than us. Leium. Leium is bigger than us. He is God's son! I know he is. I can feel it. Can't you?" Sonih pried.

Hellbound nodded in agreement.

"I can feel it. I've had dreams too. It's just too much to believe. I wasn't raised in a church. I don't know a thing about any of this stuff, Sonih," Hellbound spoke with a bold vulnerability.

Sonih grabbed his hand.

"It seems crazy, right?" Hellbound inquired.

"I guess we'll figure it out as we go," Sonih added, glowing at Hellbound.

They arrived several minutes later at a fairly new building, bordered with sidewalks, sod, and a neatly maintained flower garden. Hellbound walked around the car to the back seat to retrieve his son. He unfastened the infant car seat and began walking to the building. Hellbound knelt down next to the open car door, placed the car seat beside him, and leaned forward, placing his head on Sonih's lab and wrapping both arms around her waist. She resisted his effort momentarily. Sonih couldn't help but laugh when he kept shyly peeking up at her. She bent down and kissed his temple. Hellbound straightened to meet her lips, cradling her head with one hand.

"I love you. I love you. I love you," Hellbound whispered.

Sonih smiled sweetly and nodded knowingly. "I love you too, Jackson," Sonih added.

Hellbound raised an eyebrow and smiled at her jest. "I've not been called Jackson in a while." Hellbound laughed. "Let's find a house," Hellbound spoke as he coaxed Sonih out of the car with a gentle pull of her hand.

They walked hand in hand into the office, where they were greeted by a warmly smiling, neatly dressed, attractive woman who looked to be in her midforties. Sonih noticed the comforting smell of burning candles in the air.

"I'm Deidra, the agent assigned to help you find a home."

With the real estate agent's friendly introduction, she offered Hellbound her hand. Hellbound just stood there, frozen in a blank stare. His mind took him back to the shoot-out, during the prison break where several lost their lives, while Hellbound helplessly stood by.

"Deidra," Hellbound repeated softly in a hopeless daze, his eyes turned down to the floor in quiet remorse.

The real estate agent looked confused in how to respond. "Are you all right?" Deidra asked concerned.

Hellbound, still lost in daydreams, was silent.

Sonih pulled at his hand. "What's wrong, love?" Sonih whispered.

"Deidra was the name of one of the volunteers that died in Saudi," Hellbound answered somberly.

"With Ummi?" Sonih questioned.

Hellbound shook his head yes, knowing Sonih referred to her mom as Ummi. Sonih tightened her grip on Hellbound's hand.

"We're ready to see some homes now," Sonih stated kindly.

Deidra dropped her extended hand to her side and nodded up and down in agreement.

The young couple followed Deidra's black SUV with their borrowed tan Chevy Impala. The first model they saw was a small three-bedroom brick home. It had one small bathroom, a finished walkout basement, and a small fenced-in backyard. The yard was poorly maintained, but the structure of the house and roof was solid. The wallpaper that covered the home was old and peeling; the carpets were in need of replacement as well. The fixture and decorations were aged at least forty years, but the large appliances looked new.

"There's a small stream just a few yards off the backyard, and the owner says it's very scenic and attracts lots of wildlife," the agent informed.

Hellbound trailed around the home, inspecting every inch.

"We can fix this up," he told Sonih quietly.

"I think so too. I like it," Sonih whispered to Hellbound.

"How much is the asking price?" Hellbound questioned of Deidra.

"Eighty-five thousand," Deedra answered promptly.

"I'd pay eighty thousand if they'd replace the carpeting and cover all closing costs," Hellbound offered.

"Do you want to put that in writing?" Deidra questioned.

With her question, Hellbound turned to Sonih, who in turn nodded in agreement.

Hellbound's offer received several counter requests from the seller. Each offer was countered by Hellbound by the original offer of eighty thousand, closing costs, and replacement of all carpeting. Finally, after lingering for over two weeks, it was reluctantly accepted by the previous owners. After months of inspections and red tape, Hellbound and Sonih moved in a minuscule amount of belongings. The Jacobs generously gave the furniture from Hellbound and Sonih's basement loft. They were also surprised when a shipped box of personals arrived from Germany, after only a week of inhabitance. Hellbound was elated with a visit from Will a week later. Upon reuniting, the men embraced with a seeded love, trust, and respect. After being coarsened by Hellbound, Will decided to say a couple weeks to help fix up the house. After two weeks of relentless labor, the house was turned into a warm and welcoming home. Before returning to Germany, Will gave the young couple a generous finical gift of five thousand dollars.

Sonih would wake in the morning enchanted by the fall air and wrestle amongst the comforter to find her lover. Hellbound would watch Sonih sleep sometimes, resisting an audible laugh at the sight of Sonih sleeping. She would sleep with a content, relaxed smile frequently interrupted by a variety of awkward facial expressions and garbled words, which greatly amuzed Hellbound.

A COUNTRY LOST IN MOURNING

Back in Tabuk, Saudi Arabia, Pirum Hami grew bitter with vengeance fixated on Sonih. Field soldiers had concluded that Sonih's disappearance and involvement with Hellbound was at her own will, and thus she was viewed as a traitor. There was a public mourning for Mama Dai after her death, which lasted six days and nights. On the seventh day, they put her in the ground. The actual events surrounding her death were not released to the public. The local papers depicted the noble woman being kidnapped from her home and shot brutally in open retaliation of the Tabukin beliefs. The death of the beloved Mama Dai had spiraled a caustic revolt against all that apposed the culture, especially Germany, who was actively trying to demolish this growing clan. Outwardly, the Tabukian militia clung to their strict religious traditions and close family interactions; but inwardly, plans were made for a sinister uprising. The soldiers' count doubled to over a thousand in number, but their names and faces were hidden within the town. Behind every checkout counter and within the realm of every local oil field and factory were men with the spirit of conquest. They tasted the blood of vengeance on their tongue and dreamed of a victory that was not their own. Jehem, Timus, and the four sons of the Pirum were scattered about the country and later the globe in search of Sonih since after the conclusion of the morning with little leads.

Sonih was now being sought out for prosecution under law of treason. Sonih's name was given to Saudi government officials as the rebel culprit accountable for the attack on the German volunteers. Saudian officials took the story as fact and intern offered the escaped youth to the Germans as the sacrificial lamb of global peace.

"My heart is troubled. I cannot believe what my daughter has done, you must understand that after her sister died, she was very angry. She struggled to process right and wrong and wanted to blame someone for the pain of her death," Pirum stated as he cleared his throat, and he hung his head in sorrow, shaking it side to side with unbelief, with a weak attempt at an emotional expression.

The Saudi secretary of defense and long personal friend of Pirum Hami walked over to offer a comforting hand on his shoulder.

"I know it was difficult for you to come here today. Your family has experienced so much loss, dear friend. I will do what I can to keep Sonih safe from the punishment of treason, but it may be difficult since Germany was a formal ally to us since the world peace conference of 2006. Regardless, we have to bring her into custody until this is resolved," the secretary of defense, Bomier Yamen, spoke somberly, trying to comfort Pirum.

"No," Pirum voiced back with strong emotion. "She must pay for her crimes. We are all accountable, Bomier, not just the disadvantaged. If she is allowed, this sin then all of Saudi's youth will see it as permission to commit similar crimes. We must think of Saudi's future, not just our own. She has not only shamed her family but devastated the world, making other nations question the deep values of our Saudi nation," Pirum Hami informed his old friend.

"You are wise in many ways, but she may be clouded by the passions of youth," Secretary Bomier Yamen questioned of the girl's accusations.

"We have never hidden behind such excuses before. I would be wary of how much you bend, Bomier, for the whole world watches how our nation handles its radicals. The law was not written in gray, my friend. It was written in black and white and paid for by the blood of our countrymen. If our country bends at the whim of a child, then their sacrifices were for nothing. I will not undo a nation, Bomier, not with my own blood," Pirum spoke calmly, making steady eye contact with Secretary Bomier Yamen.

Secretary Yamen shook his head with acknowledgment and gave Pirum a customary hug, adding, "I have much to think about tonight. I have meeting with the Germany's antiterrorism committee in the morning. Please, friend, pray for my strength and wisdom in making this difficult discussion."

Secretary Yamen concluded as Pirum backed out of the secretary's office, bowed his head acceptingly, and closed the door behind him.

As Pirum left the government building, he noticed several missed cell phone calls and a message left. Pirum had turned off the phone to allow for privacy and deep discussion during his meeting with Secretary Yamen. He quickly found the calls to be from his military council, Jahem Reah. The message was hurried and demanding immediate response. Pirum quickly dialed Jahem for an update. Jahem answered the call in midsentence.

"Found her. Sir, I've found her. I've been following all flights leaving local airports around that time frame. I've seen her from afar. It's her, Pirum. She's with the young man who took Mama Dia," Jahem spoke anxiously.

The line was silent for several moments.

"Sir, are you still there?" Jahem assured.

"Yes, sorry, Jahem. Where is she?" Pirum questioned.

"The United States, Pirum. Ohio," Jahem promptly answered.

"Has she seen you?" Pirum asked.

"No," Jahem responded.

"I don't know if we have government cooperation yet, Jahem," Pirum spoke blankly. "I want to make her pay for her betrayal. She has disgraced the country and made a mockery of my teachings. Her mom's blood is on her hands, Jahem," Pirum spoke, his voice growing increasing short and deeply pitched with anger.

"The penalty for treason is great, Pirum," Jahem reminded.

"This child fears no death, Jahem. Sonih will never know the suffering she has caused her people and her family," Pirum concluded angrily.

"She has a baby," Jahem offered.

Pirum was silent again for several moments before responding. "Not only a traitor but a harlot, Jahem. We'll take the baby, Jahem, then we will start to repay some of the pain caused to us," Pirum spoke with daggers.

"Now, sir?" Jahem clarified.

"No, stay out of sight for now. I want to see what our government's next step is, they desire repentance from Germany, and she may bring it to them, Jahem," Pirum concluded.

"Yes, sir," Jahem spoke formally, ending the sinister conversation.

The next afternoon, Pirum received an update on the peace meetings between Saudi and Germany from a government informant. The Saudi government formally pressed charges against Sonih, for treason and murder. The German government was resistant to settle on this conclusion, noticing several inconsistencies between the German victims' story and Saudi's. The debate took all morning as Saudi presented a large amount of fraudulent evidence against Sonih in involvement of the crime. Finally, Germany settled on peace terms. Saudi agreed to allow German military to put up a temporary site and allowed open investigation into Saudi's affairs. Also, Germany demanded custody of Sonih Hami until their investigations had concluded. Saudi officials negotiated a time line of no longer than six months for internal investigations. After time expired, German government would be required to leave and no longer have the cooperation of Saudi's government.

THE TOURNAMENT

After two months at their new home, Hellbound received an unexpected call from Austin, who had excitedly informed him that both he and Hellbound had been invited into a MMA tournament in Toyoko.

"Come on, kid. Dom Caishon is going to be there. Neither one of you has been beaten in the octagon. A lot of people have been waiting to see you challenge him," Austin eagerly coaxed his friend.

"When is it? I've not been really been seriously working out in months," Hellbound asked.

"November 28. We've still got over two months to get ready, and the organization is footing the plane tickets and hotel," Austin informed.

"I don't know about leaving Sonih and the baby. He's still so little. How long will we be gone?" Hellbound questioned.

"Five days max," Austin blurted. "Come on, Hellbound, This is a big one. A lot of people will be watching," Austin continued to coax.

"I'll talk to Sonih and call you tomorrow," Hellbound finalized.

"Dom Caishon," Austin blurted out.

"Bye," Hellbound emphasized before ending their call.

Sonih was supportive of the trip and felt comfortable and safe in the new home, but Hellbound insisted she and Leium stay with Jenna and Alan while he was gone. Hellbound started working out with a new intensity. He had longed to challenge Dom Caishon in the octagon. Dom was in Hellbound's weather-weight division and had taken the championship for the last two years. They just never seemed to hook up at the same tournaments. This was going to be a huge challenge for Hellbound, but he thrived in the anticipation of it. Austin was en route to Ohio and was going to train with Hellbound for the two months prior to the Toyoko tournament.

TRAINING

After nearly another month, Hellbound and Austin had finalized their training and now prepared for their trip. Hellbound had to stop off for a weekly meeting with Brenten McAnthany, the state social worker, on the way to the airport. They had become increasing friendly during the past several months, and Brenten's trust of Sonih's safety continued to grow.

"Where is she? She usually comes with you," Brenten inquired.

"At home, she wanted a pass this time. Hope it's not a problem?" Hellbound explained.

"Make sure she comes next time," Brenten emphasized.

"Sure, McAnthany," Hellbound complied. "Well, I got to go. I've got a meeting to get to," Hellbound explained with a smirk and an eagerness for the door.

"Meeting? What business are you in?" Brenten inquired.

"Human relations," Hellbound responded with an unsure tone after brief hesitation then smiled back at Brenten.

"Well, I hope it's got health insurance because Sonih would be off state Medicaid in another month, since we've thus far been unable to determine citizenship," Brenten blurted as Hellbound v-lined for the door.

Hellbound paused briefly. "Leium still covered, right?" Hellbound clarified.

"Yes," Brenten called to Hellbound, following the youth out the door. Brenten reinforced with the young man.

"See ya next Friday," Hellbound yelled back as he walked backward down the hall, pushing himself into the stairwell.

Brenten just shook his head. "I don't get paid enough," Brenten softly spoke to himself before he turned back to his office, noticing a small audience of awaiting clients lined in chairs along the hall. He blushed, smiled awkwardly, and ducked back into his office.

Within two hours' time, Austin and Hellbound boarded an international flight to Toyoko. Hellbound was whirlwound between feelings of excitement, nervousness, and fear of leaving Sonih again. The excitement erupted upon arriving in Toyoko. The city was enormous with explosions of neon lights brightening the night sky. People moved busily up and down the sidewalks—hailing cabs, biking, walking, and riding electric scooters to their next venture. Hellbound was curious to find how petite many of the Japanese people were and in comparison how big he felt. He laughed to himself as he slung a large duffel bag over one shoulder using the opposite hand to tow a large-wheeled suitcase. As Hellbound stood, absorbing the sights of the town, Austin prodded insistently at his shoulder. Hellbound turned to his friend, whose stare was directing him toward the street. Hellbound turned to the street and found a classy, white extended limousine-style Hummer hidden within the overfilled meniscus of noise, traffic, people, and lights. In front of the Hummer stood a beautiful, slender, young Japanese woman with nothing in excess except heels, bust, and mounded, shiny, black hair.

She held a sign, waist-high, that read, "Jackson Harrington and Austin Ravant." She swayed her hips side to side erotically, teasing onlookers with a seductive smile.

"That's us!" Austin called as he tripped over his feet clumsily, trying to get to the Hummer and its intriguing driver.

Hellbound laughed at his friend's awkward behavior and followed him to the Hummer. Her eyes met Austin's and held his gaze before coyly requesting to see identification. As Austin fumbled through his duffel bag, she looked Hellbound up and down. She bit her bottom lip seductively as her overemphasized gaze settled on his manhood. She smiled softly while Hellbound rolled his eyes, unimpressed by her advances and instead offered his identification. Hellbound and Austin jumped into the Hummer to find a chilling bottle of champagne and a flat-screen TV. The two friends looked at each other and laughed excitedly. The driver dropped them off at a nearby hotel and informed them that they'd receive a tour of the training areas and octagon at seven tomorrow. The two nodded and thanked the driver.

"Is there anything else I can do for you?" the sexy, young driver suggested.

"No." Hellbound interrupted before Austin could open his mouth.

When Austin shot Hellbound a look of disapproval, Hellbound said, "We should keep focused, yes, Coach?"

Austin just turned away still in a blank stare.

Soon they were settled into joining hotel rooms. Hellbound crashed onto his bed, stuffed pillows behind his head, flipped on the TV, and called Sonih on the landline. The talked for hours before he finally fell to sleep, phone in hand, and fully dressed. He awoke in the morning to the sound of a dial tone and Austin knocking on the joining door.

"Hellbound! We've got to leave in ten minutes," Austin yelled from behind the closed door.

"All right!" Hellbound called back, groggily rubbing his face.

The two were treated like royalty during the trip. They walked through the arena and were updated on what the broadcasting expectations were. This was Hellbound's first televised tournament. He wasn't nervous about the fight; his only fear was the vulnerability of Sonih at home and the immense distance between them.

2020.11.16

PUNISHMENT

"The men left," Jahem updated Pirum of Sonih's status. "I followed them to the airport yesterday. It was an international flight," Jahem continued.

"The Germans demanded custody of Sonih while they sorted out the details. They said they couldn't find substantial evidence linking Sonih to the kidnappings and wouldn't support such extreme punishment of a youth regardless of convictions. I was hoping the government would take care of her for us, but since foreign affairs have become involved, our country's sense of accountability has been dulled and twisted. It looks like we need to take her, before the military finds her. It won't be long, Jahem," Pirum updated.

"What shall we do, sir?" Jehem questioned.

"I'll be there in the morning. I'm coming to get my little girl," Pirum voiced vindictively.

FIGHT AND FLIGHT

Hours later, the phone rang, and Sonih ran excitedly to retrieve it.

"Hello," Sonih chimed.

"Sweetheart," Hellbound called from the other end of the line drowned with the noise of people and an echoing loudspeaker in the background. "My match is coming up, baby. Do you have the TV on and recording?" Hellbound yelled above the noise.

"Yes, we're all hovered around the TV, but I'm not sure if I can stand to watch it," Sonih answered.

"I'll be fine, sweets, and I'm going to the airport after the tournament and should be back to you by the time you wake in the morning. I miss you, Sonih," Hellbound spoke comfortingly.

"I miss you too, love. I can't wait to see you," Sonih said.

"Well, I better get back to warming up. See ya soon, baby," Hellbound replied warmly.

"Good luck, love," Sonih responded. Sonih felt an ache of longing to be near Hellbound.

Sonih snuggled into the arm on the sofa and cradled Leium. Alan, Jenna, and Thomas were eagerly awaiting the match. Hellbound and Dom fought with unbelievable intensity and skill, tirelessly combating into the second round. Sonih and the Jacobs roared with excitement, when they watched Hellbound spin Dom into a tight lock. The competitors fought tirelessly until the third round, where Hellbound triumphed after locking Dom in a solid choke hold.

Hellbound leaped excitedly around the octagon, surrounded by the screams of excited fans. His thoughts were with Sonih. After the match, he showered quickly and excitedly went to office to claim his prize check. Austin had already hailed a cab out back, away from the hurry of the crowds. Austin's flight to Germany wouldn't leave until morning, but Hellbound had a flight to catch to United States tonight. Austin congratulated Hellbound again, and likewise, Hellbound congratulated Austin on his successful match earlier in the evening. Hellbound waved goodbye as he ducked into the cab. Hellbound, still bursting with adrenaline, was talking breathlessly about the events of the fight to the uninterested cabby. Hellbound hurried through the airport to his terminal and checked in with the attendant. Hellbound anxiously paced the corridor, awaiting his boarding call.

SURPRISE AT HOME

Sonih woke up to a nuzzling kiss on the face. She laughed with excitement as she grabbed Hellbound and pulled him next to her in the bed.

"You won," Sonih beamed proudly.

Hellbound just laughed as he wiggled beneath the sheets for a long-awaited reunion.

"I won before I even left. I love you," Hellbound whispered.

"I love you too," Sonih smiled through the dark of the basement.

They slept for only an hour before they woke to the babbling of the baby.

"Let's go home," Hellbound suggested.

"Yes, I want to go home," Sonih agreed.

They walked into their cozy, suburban home to find the flashing light of the answering machine. Hellbound played the messages. The first one was from their caseworker, Brenten. He was anxiously demanding a callback.

"Jackson, there was a missing person report filed, and Sonih fits the description. Her dad is here with birth certificates, legal papers, and lawyers. We're going to have to settle this ASAP! Call me," Brenten's recorded voice rang through the speaker.

"My dad?" Sonih panicked as Hellbound grabbed the phone hastily.

Sonih tearfully overheard a one-sided conversation.

"This is Jackson," Hellbound spoke into the phone. "When?" Hellbound barked into the receiver. "Do we need a lawyer?" Hellbound questioned, followed by moments of silence.

Finally, after a series of additional questioning, Hellbound said, "We'll see you Monday morning." Hellbound ended the call, and then he proceeded to hang up the phone gently, as if it would break.

"What'd he say?" Sonih wept.

"Your dad's here. He's demanding custody of you. He refuses to allow you emancipation. He's got lawyers. Brenten said since you're nearing age, the judge will most likely grant emancipation anyway. He does recommend we bring a lawyer, just to be safe. Brenten says there is going to be an informal meeting, Monday morning."

MONDAY

Sonih knew her presence was mandatory, but she was filled with fear. Hellbound held Sonih close.

"We've got to legally break free of him. I won't let him hurt you," Hellbound consoled Sonih, and he gently stroked her hand as they waited in the familiar hallway outside of Brenten's office.

Their lawyer arrived and joined Hellbound and Sonih. After twenty devastating minutes, Brenten exited his office and called Hellbound, Sonih, and their lawyer to follow him to the conference room, down the hall.

The hard soles of Sonih's heels echoed down the hallway. Brenten pushed open the solid white door to reveal Pirum, who was accompanied by two lawyers, already sitting at the conference table. Sonih held her breath at the sight of her father, and chills traveled through her. Sonih straightened her posture and looked at her father in a requited, cold vengeance. Pirum and his American lawyers stood with respect while the newcomers took their seats. The suspense hung eerily in the room as Brenten fumbled through paperwork.

"OK, let's begin," Brenten voiced after clearing his throat and smiling nervously at the foreign visitor.

Suddenly, the door swung open, and Judge Kenedi walked in. "Sorry I'm late."

The prim female judge smiled as she entered the room. Her hair was curled neatly and hung chin-length. Her glasses were dainty and gray pinstriped skirt-suit, which was perfectly ironed. She sat next to social worker Brenten McAnthany and crossed her legs, placing a notepad on the table in front of her. Brenten noticed the sketched notes and questions on the judge's notepad reflected the current proceedings.

"Judge Kenedi, it's always wonderful to see you, but I was under the impression this was an informal gathering to sort out the facts," Brenten clarified with Judge Kenedi.

"No sense dragging this out. I was notified of the situation, and if I sit in now, we can all sift through the information and not have to spend extra time and cost of coming back," Judge Kenedi informed confidently, and she scanned the room for any opposition.

Hellbound and Sonih tightened the grip of their hands, and both sat dumbfounded by this new blow.

"I'll start, if it's all right?" one of Pirum's American lawyers questioned of the judge.

"Sure," Judge Kenedi dictated with a smile.

"I'll start with the girl's birth certificate that verifies my client is her father and also that states that Saudi Arabia is her country of origin and she snuck into the States illegally," Pirum's lawyer stated while he handed a small stack of papers to Judge Kenedi.

The judge took several minutes to clarify the paperwork.

"Is this your father, young lady?" the judge asked Sonih.

Sonih looked desperately into the judge's eyes.

"Yes, ma'am, he is, but I am afraid of him. He's a dangerous man, and he killed my twin sister three years ago. I won't go with him," Sonih demanded.

"Well, young lady, Mr. McAnthany can help hook you both up with an overseas child welfare service to ensure your safety," the judge kindly spoke to Sonih.

"No, please," Sonih shouted as she rose to her feet in opposition.

"Miss, I can imagine how devastating it must be to have survived the tragic death of a twin and also your mother. I have looked through the death certificates and taken the initiative of talking to several government officials and physicians that are familiar with your family and its losses. Sonih, they all feel your dad is an honorable and good man, who was in no way responsible for their deaths. I think it would be wise to talk to a psychologist who can help you sort through all these feelings," Judge Kenedi spoke flatly.

"No," Hellbound cried. "She's my wife, we have a son," Hellbound emphasized.

"Sir, I appreciate your wonderful care in guardianship of Sonih. But at the end of the day, Jackson, she is underage, an illegal alien without marriage certificate or even the legal ability to make a decision of marriage. I'm afraid I have no choice but to return the girl to her home," Judge Kenedi spoke bluntly.

Hellbound jumped from his chair in defiance of her remarks, causing the chair to fall back against the wall.

"Sir, I suggest you be seated before I have you put in jail," Judge Kenedi scolded.

Hellbound paused briefly before repositioning his chair from the ground and carefully lowering himself into the chair; his face was still red with anger.

"And what of the infant?" Pirum's attorney questioned.

"If the dad's of legal age, he'll obtain custody. We'll just need a simple DNA sample from both parents to verify parentage," Judge Kenedi informed.

"Judge Kenedi, our client wishes to press charges of statutory rape against Mr. Herrington," one of the attorneys arrogantly informed the judge.

"Mr. Hami, doctors date conception time back to when Sonih was in Saudi Arabia. That is way out of my jurisdiction, sir. But if such a law exists in Saudi, then by all means you may peruse with the law enforcement there," Judge Kenedi spoke back promptly. "You will both be required to submit a simple mouth swab for DNA testing. A lab technician will be over to your home in the morning," Judge Kenedi emphasized to Hellbound while holding steady eye contact, "to collect a swab from both of you and the infant."

"And what if it turns out Mr. Herrington is not the biological father?" Pirum's attorney directed toward the judge.

"Then the infant will be released to Mr. Hami's custody," the judge informed.

"I won't submit a DNA sample, I'll die first," Sonih cried.

Sonih abruptly sprung to her feet and raced to the door. Hellbound sprinted behind her. They raced down the wooden stairs before their exit was blocked at the stairwell exit by a security guard who grabbed Sonih firmly by the shoulders. Hellbound pushed the unexpected guard, causing his grip on Sonih to fail. The two burst out of the stairwell and into the lobby where two police officers were waiting.

"Don't resist, son," one police urged as he approached Hellbound.

Hellbound stopped.

"You're not under arrest, kid. We just have to make sure we get this situation is settled with as little dispute as possible," the policeman informed while cuffing Hellbound's hands behind his back.

The elevator opened, and Pirum, his attorneys, Brenten McAnthany, and the judge stepped out. Sonih wept at Hellbound's feet, and he respectively said, "I love you, Sonih."

Pirum grabbed Sonih by the arm, pulling her to her feet and dragging her toward the door. Sonih screamed, "No," and wiggled free of Pirum's grasp, ran over to Hellbound, and wrapped her arms around his neck.

"I love you, always," Sonih whispered as she kissed his lips. "Take care of Leium. Don't let my dad get him, no matter what. He'll turn him cold and hateful, like my brothers," Sonih whispered.

"I'll take good care of him, love," Hellbound responded weakly as tears filled his eyes.

"Do I need to have one of these police officers escort you, Sonih?" Pirum threatened of Sonih.

Sonih took a deep breath and pulled herself away from Hellbound. Sonih smiled lovingly at Hellbound and bravely walked to the chauffeured car out front, as directed by Pirum. She looked back one last time at Hellbound and smiled deeply. She felt overcome with love for him. Sonih then slipped into the back seat of the car, and the chauffer promptly shut the door behind her.

Pirum stood in the lobby.

"Have the lab technician stop by the hotel in the morning before we leave for Saudi. I'll make sure Sonih consents," Pirum spoke to the judge with a manufactured smile. "If for some reason he's not the father, we'll send for the infant later," Pirum clarified with Judge Kenedi.

"OK, we'll keep you updated, but we will look for follow-up with your human services agency and psychologist treatment in Saudi to ensure compliance," the judge demanded.

Brenten stood frozen in his tracks as Pirum left the building and joined Sonih in the car.

"I'm sorry," Brenten meekly called to Hellbound. "I didn't think it would be like this. I'm sorry, Jackson," Brenten repeated.

Hellbound could not see Brenten through his anger. He could not see his incompetent lawyer through the grave disappointment. He only saw the car drive away and felt the uncontrollable tears trickle down his cheeks. The police waited a few moments to assess Hellbound's reactions before confidently unlocking the cuffs from his wrists. Hellbound walked out of the building alone, feeling lost and helpless, covered by a disorientating fog of the nightmare that surrounded him.

"I'm going to get my son," Hellbound voiced angrily as he pushed out the main entranceway doors.

The lobby was silent as its captives were at a loss for words. Then Brenten looked at Judge Kenedi with deep disgust.

"Do you really think that was the right thing to do?" Brenten voiced sarcastically.

"It was the only thing we could do," Judge Kenedi justified.

"You judge! It was the only thing you could do. This girl's death will haunt you," Brenten spoke snidely as he too left the building.

2020.11.31

TAKEOFF

The next morning, Hellbound woke to the chime of the doorbell. He was spread out awkwardly on the sofa and felt surprised that he fell asleep during the restless night that preceded. He opened the door while rubbing the sleep from his eyes. The lab technician introduced herself formally as Hellbound gestured her inside. Hellbound went to retrieve Leium from his crib while the technician pulled her equipment from her suitcase. She professionally explained the "simple and painless" procedure of collecting DNA. She had Hellbound sign paper authorizing consent to treatment and release of information for the purpose of establishing paternity of Leium. After a few quick mouth swabs, she placed the labeled specimens in a small cooler and excused herself to the door.

The same technician's next stop was the hotel, where Sonih, Pirum, and his men temporarily stayed. The technician cheerfully knocked at the door before repeating her introduction. Pirum asked her to come in. The technician saw Sonih sitting expressionless on the sofa.

"I'll just need a painless oral swab to verify maternity of Leium," the technician explained.

Sonih leaped to her feet, tackled the technician, and shoved her to the ground.

"No!" Sonih yelled at the technician erratically, before Pirum and his men could pull Sonih off the lab tech.

"Fine, leave the little bastard here. You'll never see his face again," Pirum yelled at Sonih while the tech scrambled out the door fearfully.

Within the hour, Sonih boarded a private jet, along with her father and flight crew and headed to Saudi Arabia.

Two Weeks Later

"Mr. Herrington," a voice called over the receiver of Hellbound's phone.

"Yes," Hellbound answered.

"This is Dr. Steven Carter. I'm head of the forensic lab at Saint Lawerence Hospital. Understand please, that my call today is entirely confidential. We've discovered some abnormalities in the DNA testing, and we're hoping to clarify things with you," the serious-toned doctor explained.

"Shoot," Hellbound coaxed.

"Well, Ms. Hami wouldn't submit her DNA, but—" the doctor started before being interrupted.

"Mrs. Herrington, or Sonih, Doctor," Hellbound annoyingly corrected.

"Sorry, Sonih wouldn't allow us to take a DNA sample to compare, but the father..." the doctor began to stutter nervously.

"What?" Hellbound prompted.

"Well, there's only one set of DNA. It's not possible. Everyone have variations of two strands of DNA—one from mom and one from dad," Dr. Carter explained.

"An error, right? Do you need another sample from Leium?" Helbound asked.

"Of course, we'll rerun the studies, but the sample wasn't compromised, and the present strand is flawless. I've literally never seen anything like this in the fifteen years I've worked with DNA," Dr. Carter emphasized.

"What exactly are you telling me, Doctor?" Hellbound questioned.

"I am confident a repeated study will show identical results. All logic states that this is an impossibility. If this is proven true, Mr. Harrington, it would be a revolutionary find," Dr. Carter emphasized.

"Does the DNA strand match mine?" Hellbound asked hopefully.

"No, Mr. Herrington it does not match, but yours, surprisingly, is also missing a whole DNA strand," the doctor spoke abruptly. "I'm sorry, but it doesn't match," Dr. Carter apologized. "Mr. Herrington?" the doctor carter called.

"Yeah?" Hellbound inquired.

"Don't mention this call to anyone, OK?" the doctor recommended.

"Sure," Hellbound promptly responded before hanging up the receiver.

Days later, an expected call from Brenten McAnthany requesting a repeat oral swab along with blood samples from Leium. Hellbound complied with the request, and another lab technician was in his home within the hour. Hellbound was fearful about what this might mean for him and Leium. Hellbound had given his word to Sonih that Leium would never be given to Pirum. The thought haunted him. What if Sonih was forced to submit DNA and Pirum took custody of Leium? He worried about Sonih's safety and dreamed of her each night.

The next series of DNA tests resulted within days and were released back to the human welfare office and in turn back to Hellbound. He met with Brenten McAnthany regarding about the findings.

"Jackson, I think everyone will be astonished at the results. Pirum assumed you'd be named the father, but understand we legally have to inform him of changes in the case. He may want to force Sonih to submit now. He seemed very interested in custody at the hearing," Brenten collaborated with Hellbound.

"I know. I made a promise to Sonih that Pirum would not end up with that baby, and I will keep it at all costs," Hellbound emphasized.

"We're helpless." Brenten pleaded.

"You're helpless, Brenten," Hellbound called as he quickly exited the office.

That night Hellbound quickly packed necessities into old gym bags and boxed up nonperishable foods and went to the store and purchased an excess of infant formulas, baby food, diapers, and wipes. He packed Jenna's SUV up with supplies. The next morning, he woke early and got himself and Leium ready when he heard the doorbell. He peeked cautiously through the peephole within the door. Hellbound leaped with excitement while he swung the door open.

"Sonih!" Hellbound screamed while tacking his visitor into a tight hug.

He bounced around the front yard before hearing her call assertively, "No," as she wiggled free and landed a punch on Hellbound's jaw that caused his head to jolt backward. She backed away from Hellbound a few steps.

"I'm not Sonih," she yelled, while trying to catch her breath. She extended her hand out toward him. "I'm Korih," she spoke with a smile.

Hellbound's jaw dropped in disbelief.

"Sonih said you were dead," Hellbound questioned while shaking his head in opposition.

"I was dead on the operating table for three minutes and was in critical condition for months afterward. The kind doctor who cared for me couldn't stand the thought of releasing me back into the home that had nearly killed me. He was the same doctor who fraudulently signed the death certificate. He hid me all this time, educated me, fed me, kept me safe. Sonih's condition was less serious, so her death would've been well investigated. He's kept me informed of Sonih's life. I just wanted her to be happy and safe. Now she needs my help," Korih spoke with wisdom, grace, and confidence.

"How can you help?" Hellbound asked.

"I know my sister. She wouldn't want her son with our father. He's a barbarian of the worst sort, and the people love him. They've told my father of the findings, and he's going to force Sonih to test. He wants that baby. Just for spite, he'll turn that baby into what we despise the most. We'll convince them I'm Leium's mother, and it won't be contested," Korih spoke knowledgably.

"They'll want a DNA test," Hellbound interjected skeptically.

"Exactly," Korih said while smiling. "Our DNA is the same, and Korih Hami is dead. Pirum has no rights to me and thus no rights to Leium. Leium's not going anywhere," Korih smiled to Hellbound.

Hellbound tried to absorb the situation and play out all possible outcomes in his mind. Hellbound's face was grimaced with confusion before he spoke.

"This may work," Hellbound spoke unsurely.

The next day, they presented the scenario as rehearsed. Korih had changed her superficial appearance as much as possible with colored hair, sunglasses, detailed makeup, and a wild dress and jewelry. Korih acted the part brilliantly, stating she had returned to India for a visit briefly before returning for her infant son. The blood tests promptly came back in her favor, and custody was granted to Korih—or as the courts knew her, "Miah Demont." She was allowed temporary citizenship to the United States. They went the same day to submit request for legal adoption of Leium in Jackson's name.

ARRANGED MARRIAGE

Korih kept in close contact with the Dr. Randal Rian, the kind doctor that saved her life and had kept her hidden for years from her father's grasp. Randal had contacts within the society and was well informed of upcoming plans. On such a call, Korih frantically paced the living room.

"When?" Korih demanded of the caller. "We're going to have to move up our rescue plans."

Korih called to Hellbound while hanging up the phone. Hellbound looked at Korih with questioning eyes.

"Pirum's arranged a marriage for Sonih. Some dirty old politician, no doubt, so Father can gain better control of Saudi's government," Korih spoke with disgust.

"Over my dead body!" Hellbound voiced furiously. "We're going to need a plan to get her back home, yesterday," Hellbound spoke with rage, while restlessly stomping around the house. "When?" Hellbound asked, fearing Korih's response.

She looked up at him somberly. "We've got seven days," Korih responded.

"We can have the German Army take her into custody," Hellbound thought out loud.

"No, she's been cleared of father's fraudulent charges, and Germany is attempting to resolve terrorism. They're not going to start any fires with the biggest private military in Saudi," Korih spoke knowledgeably.

"She's gotta see a shrink. We'll see if we can get Will in the country and have Brenten coordinate her to hook up with him," Hellbound suggested.

"That's a long shot, and Pirum is very suspicious of foreigners. He'll never allow her to see Will professionally," Korih reasoned. "There's only one way that I can see that this is going to work," Korih boasted confidently.

Hellbound cocked his head toward Korih and furrowed his brow with intrigue.

INTERVENTION

"Did you hear, child, Leium's not even yours," Pirum said, laughing annoyingly toward Sonih.

Sonih tried to hide her expression of confusion.

"Some Indian woman claimed the baby was hers, and DNA testing agreed," Pirum spoke, still amused by the update. "What, were you watching the baby, or did you steal him? My, I'll be glad when you're married off, child. You're a headache and a harlot, you're lucky someone even wanted to marry you. Maybe he'll have better luck keeping you in line. Get ready, you have an appointment with Dr. Rian to make sure you don't have any sex diseases before you marry."

Pirum looked at Sonih with disgust before walking out the door and muttering, "Harlot," under his breath. Sonih was quiet and somber. She knelt aside her bed and prayed as the late preacher had taught her. When she rose, it was with a renewed strength. She redressed for her doctor appointment.

Less than an hour later, Sonih was waiting in the familiar office of Dr. Rian, the doctor who had saved her so many years ago. Dr. Randal Rian had deep compassion for Sonih, and she called him "friend." An older, smiling nurse called Sonih's name, and she rose and followed the nurse through the maze of hallways into a private room where she was asked to take off her clothes and change into a bland brown dress with head cover. Sonih thought the request was unusual but complied without question. The nurse then led her to

Dr. Rian's office, where he was already waiting. When she saw his face, she raced to him, wrapping her arms around him in a sincere hug.

"Friend, I'm so glad to see you," Sonih beckoned.

Randal just smiled at the young girl with pride, stood, and walked over to the closet door. He swung open the closet door, and Korih stepped out, smiling to capacity. Sonih began to cry and laughed in an uncontrollable whirlwind of emotion. Korih laughed with deep happiness, and they reunited into a smoldering hug.

"You're not dead," Sonih cried.

"Randal saved me and kept me hidden from the family. He said your condition was stable and would have spiraled an investigation. We've been watching from a distance and making sure you're safe," Korih explained to Sonih.

"I've missed you so much," Sonih spoke with tears of joy still streaming down her face.

"I've missed you," Korih requited, tightening her hug on Sonih and kissing her cheek.

"I'm never going to let you go again," Sonih muttered. "Me and you, together we're strong," Sonih continued, still laughing with joy.

Korih smiled bravely as tears welled up in her eyes.

"Sonih, we only have a few minutes," Korih voiced as she forced a weak smile on her face.

Sonih looked Korih over and noticed she was wearing the same attire that Sonih had worn to the appointment. Sonih's face filled with fear as she started saying, "No," respectively in a soft, tear-soaked moan, grabbing Korih's arms in resistance.

"This moment may be the only reason I didn't die that night. I have a strong feeling Leium is going to help a lot of people. He's going to be amazing. I know it, Sonih, and he needs his mom," Korih calmly rationed.

Sonih grabbed Korih into a tight hug and was at a loss for words.

"How do you know?" Sonih cried.

"I have a wonderfully vivid dream. It was the most unusual dream I've ever had, and it kept reoccurring. I saw you holding a baby and smiling as angels danced in the skies above you. Everyone was focused on the baby. I felt so small in the dream. One of the angels came to me and said, 'You have to help him, Korih. You have to help, Leium.' I was so scared, Sonih. I kept asking, 'How?' But the angels just smiled and continued to dance in the skies. I had this dream long before you even left for the United States. I knew his name would be Leium, Sonih, and that scares me," Korih explained to Sonih.

"I know, Korih, I had a similar dream frequently while I was in the coma. The angels called him Leium. They said they needed me, that Leium needed me. I was so scared in my dream that I just cowered down on the ground, but they handed him to me and said again, 'Leium needs you...'" Sonih fearfully confessed to Korih.

Korih took Sonih's hands in her own as she did the night they almost died. They bowed together, touching their heads at their hairlines.

"We need to be brave, Sonih," Korih spoke wisely.

"You're so much stronger than me," Sonih confessed.

They hugged a last deep hug, both knowing that it would most likely be the last time they saw each other.

"I have to go now, Sonih," Korih spoke bravely, regaining her composure.

Sonih's face grimaced with emotion, and she shook her head knowingly at Korih. Randal swept Korih up in a tight hug and quivered with emotion. Korih warmly requited before pulling away, reminding Dr. Rian, "It's time."

Randal kissed Korih's hairline affectionately.

"I love you, old man," Korih said as she pulled away from Randal.

Randal was twenty-seven, and eleven years her senior, as he had been a young doctor of only twenty-five on the night he saved her. He was genuine and strong, with a round face, round glasses, and giant heart. Randal ordered lovingly as he narrowed his gaze on Koriah.

"I love you, Korih," Sonih whispered as Dr. Rian coaxed her to hide in the closet. Korih nodded knowingly and smiled back at Sonih humbly before exiting the office. Dr. Rian closed the door, and Sonih was left waiting in small, dark closet until the office closed that evening.

HOME AGAIN

Randal closed the office, as he did most evenings, waving by to the last couple nurses as they filtered into the parking lot. Moments later, Sonih heard the creak of the closet door open as a stream of light consumed the dark closet. Sonih blocked the light with one hand while grimacing her face as she accommodated her eyes. Sonih eased to a stand, twisting her torso while extending her arms high above her head in an encompassing stretch.

"Are you ready, Sonny girl?" Randal kindly asked with a soft smile while offering an outreached open hand as a guide.

Sonih took his hand, and he led her through the maze of hallways into the employee break room. He retrieved a brown sac from the refrigerator and removed a couple of pita wraps, placing them in front of Sonih, in offering. He removed a preheated cup of green tea from the microwave, placing it too in front of Sonih. Sonih smiled.

"Thank you," Sonih voiced humbly.

They sat talking about Korih, trying to account for the lost time as Sonih hungrily ate a pita.

"I feel such a deep happiness, like an empty place is now filled inside me. I just can't believe that that brat swapped places with me," Sonih said laughing. "I bet it was her stubborn idea too." Sonih smiled at Randal, as he nodded in agreement.

"She's always looked after you, Sonih, even when you didn't know she was looking. She's such a powerful, amazing young woman. I will truly miss her," Randal confessed.

"Thank you," Sonih spoke genuinely as she grabbed Randal's hands with hers in comfort. "You saved her, Randal. Father would have eventually killed her. He was very intimidated by her strength. Korih had no fear for Father, and he hated that. If you don't submit to Father's will, he'll crush you. I truly hate that man. I am embarrassed to call him Father," Sonih rambled.

"Are you done?" Randal questioned, gesturing toward the pita.

"Yes," Sonih quickly answered.

"Then let's get you back home, Sonih," Randal coaxed.

They slipped through the barren parking lot to Randal's black SUV. Sonih had her face buried beneath the mounds of loose clothing of the dark head wrap. Randal spiraled the SUV through town and shortly arrived at a private airport. There awaited a private jet, headed for the USA. Randal escorted Sonih to the boarding stairs where a thin, old, bearded pilot greeted her. Upon entering the plane, she scanned her surroundings. She felt an eerie sense that someone was behind her and spun around defensively.

"Hellbound!" Sonih screamed.

"Shh," Hellbound laughed softly. "I don't think I have many friends here," Hellbound joked sarcastically.

Sonih just smiled, and the young couple melted into a consuming hug. Hellbound breathed in her familiar smell and nestled his face into the loose cloth of the headdress as tendrils of hair escaped the wrap and flooded around her face. She unhooked the headdress, exposing her face to him.

"My sister is alive," Sonih cheerfully informed Hellbound.

"I know, Sonih," Hellbound smiled.

The young lovers were lost in conversation during the flight before eventually fading to sleep, still in the security of each other's arms. They arrived at a small private airport near Dayton, Ohio. The two stumbled down the boarding ladder and were greeted by a ground crew.

"You must be Jackson?" the crew questioned of Hellbound, and he nodded, "Yes."

"And you, young lady, must be Miah?" the crew questioned, looking at Sonih.

She turned to Jackson and smiled.

"Yes, this is Miah," Jackson spoke up assertively, offering the crew both sets of IDs and passports.

"Looks like everything is in order. There are some people in the lobby waiting to pick you up. Did you have any bags to retrieve?" the crew questioned.

"Nope," Jackson answered as the crew leader shot a confused look at Hellbound.

The crew leader just shrugged carelessly and pointed the young couple toward the lobby. As Hellbound and Sonih walked arm in arm across the runway, Sonih looked up and rolled her eyes, while playfully snickering.

"Miah?" Sonih questioned.

Hellbound shook his head yes. "Miah Demont," Hellbound clarified.

"Don't you think, maybe you should have mentioned that during the sixteen-hour flight?" Sonih jested sarcastically.

Hellbound laughed, pulling Sonih to himself in a one-armed hug while they continued walking.

"Your sister had all that identification already. The doctor had it set up for her long ago," Hellbound informed.

"Dr. Rian is a wonderful man. Did you know he spent his whole life's savings on these private flights?" Hellbound voiced, shaking his head in unbelief. "For us!" Hellbound emphasized.

Sonih smiled, humbled by the thought of such a gift. "We'll never be able to pay back all those who sacrificed so much for us," Sonih spoke somberly.

Hellbound leaned down and kissed Sonih's forehead.

"I don't deserve you," Hellbound confessed.

"How did you know it was Korih and not me, when she came to the house?" Sonih questioned of Hellbound's earlier stories during the flight home.

"Because she punches," Hellbound joked, rubbing his jaw with his free hand.

Sonih erupted into laughter. "She is so feisty, right?" Sonih laughed. "I can't believe she's marrying that old politician for me. Poor Korih," Sonih muttered.

"Poor politician," Hellbound shook his head, rubbing his jaw again.

Sonih laughed again, pushing Hellbound away in offense to his comment.

"She can hold her own, can't she?" Sonih agreed.

Hellbound smiled at Sonih a nodded in acknowledgment.

The Jacobs were waiting impatiently in the lobby. Hellbound and Sonih were welcomed back with tight hugs and excitement. Sonih retrieved Leium from Jenna's arms.

"I'm home, baby," Sonih whispered to Leium while kissing his soft, chubby face.

Sonih secured him into a loving cradle while rocking him side to side.

"My baby," Sonih whispered joyfully.

"Where's Thomas?" Hellbound questioned.

"He's running around the outside of the building," Alan informed while laughing and shrugging his shoulders. "It's like he's got a jet in his butt. He doesn't stop," Alan joked playfully.

"He's got nine years' worth of energy to get out," Jenna reasoned.

Hellbound smiled at the couple's playful banter.

"Let's get her home."

Jenna encouragingly wrapped an arm around Sonih and led her to the car, while Hellbound and Alan, now talking, slowly followed. They settled into the car and secured Leium in his car seat. Alan started the car and buckled.

"Alan," Jenna scolded angrily.

Alan laughed. "I wasn't going to forget him," Alan joked. "He'd probably beat us home, anyway," Alan reasoned.

"True as that may be," Jenna said in agreement.

"Thomas!" Alan repeatedly called out the driver's side window.

The young boy appeared from behind the building and began sprinting toward the car, and Alan playfully crept down the drive. As Thomas caught up to the car, Alan stopped and swung open the driver's side door. Thomas jumped in the car, crawled across Alan's lap, and buckled into the front seat between his parents. Jenna leaned over and kissed Thomas's cheek as Alan accelerated away.

NEWLY WEDS

Alan sat smiling adoringly at Jenna as the magistrate began the ceremony. Hellbound and Sonih stood hand in hand, facing the magistrate, both smiling eagerly.

"Is there a ring?" the magistrate questioned of Hellbound.

Hellbound peered back, and Thomas popped out of his seat, quickly handing a ring box to Hellbound. Hellbound opened the box and turned it toward Sonih for approval. Sonih's jaw dropped at the beauty of the piece and how well it fitted them. It was modest in size, but it shown brightly with accenting sapphires butterflied around the modest diamond. As the noon sun filtered into a nearby window and reflected light through the ring, a cascade of twinkling spots of light spread around the room, moving about on the walls like fireflies. Sonih looked around the room, amused by the colorful prisms of light.

"I now pronounce you Mr. and Mrs. Jackson and Miah Herrington," the magistrate announced proudly.

Then Jenna, Alan, Thomas, and Will stood to their feet, clapping and cheering with excitement as the new couple shared their first kiss as husband and wife.

Sonih's lips hungrily melted into Hellbound's, and she was overcome with excitement. Hellbound stepped back from Sonih and eagerly pulled the ring from the box, fitting it onto Sonih's ring finger.

"It fits," Hellbound voiced surprised. "The lady at the antique shop said I'd probably have to get it sized because it's really small," Hellbound informed Sonih.

"It fits perfect. I've got long, narrow fingers," Sonih reassured. "Why'd you pick the opals?" Sonih questioned.

"Those stones around the diamond?" Hellbound asked naively. Sonih nodded, "Yes."

"I thought it looked good. Do you like the opals?" Hellbound questioned.

Sonih nodded, "Yes," and looked up at Hellbound surprised.

"Opals are your birth stone," Sonih educated. "October, right?" Sonih clarified.

"Yup," Hellbound answered. "That's when we celebrate it, anyway. We could never find out for certain when or where I was born," Hellbound voiced.

"I guess it was meant to be," Sonih interpreted.

"We are meant to be," Hellbound said certainly as Sonih looked smilingly up at him with pride and respect.

The day was bittersweet, for Sonih knew that, a world away, Korih was also marrying—under much different circumstances.

Korih was wearing a beautiful white bridal gown with long bead headdress. Flowers lined the aisles of the church. Their father spoke boisterously at the podium.

"It is a wonderful honor for me to preside over the wedding of my beautiful daughter, Sonih, and longtime friend, Amier Yamen. We've known brothers Amier and Bromier Yamen since they've been young and watched both grow to become noble and powerful leaders. It is with great pride that I give to you my only daughter, Sonih. I hope you live peacefully and have many beautiful children," Pirum loudly voiced.

Korih turned behind her to see the rows of podiums filled with both prestigious and common faces.

"I now present to the great nation of Saudi Arabia, Mr. and Mrs. Amier Yamen," Pirum concluded as Amier leaned down, claiming his bride by the hand, and bowing to Pirum and the crowd in traditional gratitude.

Amier led Korih into an awaiting limousine. He nestled into the seat beside Korih and ogled at her lustfully.

"Sonih, you're the most beautiful woman I've ever seen," Amier praised Sonih.

Korih rolled her eyes, unimpressed by his generic statements.

"Really, you're fat and not a bit attractive," Korih emphasized bluntly.

Amier's mouth dropped open, and he gasped, surprised by her cruel statement.

"Maybe you'll grow to love me," Amier suggested.

"Yeah, I don't think so," Korih cockily informed.

Amier was silent and turned away from Korih. "You're a crab," Amier gasped.

"I guess you won't be so superficial in the future, old man," Korih spoke with penetrating sarcasm.

"Are you hungry?" Amier questioned, sincerely holding a bottle of champagne and plate of pastries.

"Starving," Korih interrupted.

"Shame," Amier voiced, shoving a sweet, warm keiflea into his mouth and wiggling the cork from the bottle with his strong hands.

"You better give me some of that champagne at least, old man. If I'm going to be married to you, I want to be at least half lit," Korih snidely boasted back at Amier.

"You don't talk like a lady," Amier spoke confused.

"Maybe I'm not, old man," Korih suggested.

"I'm scared," Amier confessed.

"You should be," Korih stated while rolling her eyes annoyingly at Amier. "Now, let's go get something to eat, old man," Korih demanded.

Amier silently gazed off into the distance.

ENDING

Sonih and Hellbound began night classes at the community college. Hellbound worked a full-time position as a laborer at Alan's shop. Sonih stayed home with Leium during the days and babysat three neighbor children to help supplement their finances. Hellbound seldom retreated to any MMA tournaments because of his full schedule and lack of the enormous amount of time it took for training. Will frequently tried to coax them to move to Germany and live nearby but eventually gave up after repeated declines. Instead, Will moved to Ohio and accepted a position as a professor of psychology at Ohio State and treated some private patients when time allowed. Alan and Jenna continued to be supportive friends, watching Leium on the nights the couple attended night classes.

Korih called Sonih daily on the phone. Korih was safe and far from Pirum's grasp. Pirum had hoped to gain power and leverage on Saudi affairs by Sonih and Amier's union. Contradictory to Pirum's ambitions, Amier quickly became mesmerized by Korih's beauty, power, and grace. He was no longer an ally to Pirum but soon became Korih's ear, voice, and hand.

2021.5.31

MAIL

Leium's adoption finalized May 2, 2021, naming Jackson as legal father. Leium celebrated his first birthday April 31, 2021, in the quiet of a small backyard gathering. The sun fell in the sky, causing a vibrant purple sky, which twisted with a burning-red overcast. Hellbound seared the last of the bratwurst on the grill, placing them on a small plate beside the grill, before he noticed the unusual silence around him. The radio continued to play, but all voices faded. Hellbound looked around to find Jenna, Sonih, and Alan still sitting at the old woodened picnic table but hushed, staring sky, awestruck by its beauty. Thomas halted mid sprint and gazed enchanted by the mysterious blend of colors.

"Have you ever seen anything like it?" Alan asked the group as Will crept into backyard, swinging the gate open, causing a high-pitched squeak.

"No, I defiantly have not. I was talking to a colleague at the university. He teaches history and religious science. He was saying how Christians used to believe a fiery purple sky was a sign of upcoming change in the heavens. Maybe we should take warning?" Will informed as he settled into a seat at the picnic table next to Jenna.

"I think it's beautiful," Sonih added.

"Cheers to that," Jenna agreed, holding her plastic cup of pop in the air and smiling.

The group touched glasses as they began to fill their plates with brats, fresh vegetables, and potato chips.

"Oh, we forgot the ketchup," Sonih noticed while standing to her feet.

"I've got it, sweets. I have to leak, anyway," Hellbound interrupted, kissing Sonih on the lips affectionately before disappearing into the house.

After using the bathroom, Hellbound walked to the refrigerator to grab the ketchup. While standing, he noticed a small pile of unopened mail on the counter. Hellbound sat the ketchup on the counter while he sifted through the envelopes. One particular envelope caught his attention. It had no return address and was simply addressed to "Hellbound" with his corresponding address. Hellbound had never recalled seeing his nickname on an envelope before, and the writing was tiny and handwritten in perfect cursive. He tore the envelope open to find what looked to be a very old, yellowed, and brittle piece of paper. Hellbound noticed the writing on the paper did not match that on the envelope. It was written in some other language that Hellbound didn't recognize but was signed at the bottom: "Lucifer."

"What is this?" Hellbound questioned of Will, while walking into the backyard and holding the aged letter in his hand.

Will stood up with his eyes squinted with confusion. The talking around the picnic table hushed as the others picked up on the seriousness in Hellbound's tone. Will grabbed the document from Hellbound and studied it intently.

"This is Latin," Will informed. "I don't know what this is, but I bet, that colleague I was telling you about will know," Will continued.

"Latin?" Hellbound clarified.

"Yeah, I'm pretty certain this is Latin. Who would send you something like that?" Will wondered aloud.

"It was addressed to Hellbound not Jackson Herrington," Hellbound announced. "Someone's messing with me," Hellbound suspected. "Did you see the signature?" Hellbound questioned Will.

Will nodded yes somberly.

"What? Who's it from?" Sonih asked concerned.

The men stood silent, staring at each other.

"Who?" Sonih demanded of Hellbound.

"Lucifer." Hellbound answered abruptly.

Sonih's eyes were distant and deep, as her face cringed in confusion.

"The devil," Jenna clarified. "It was Satan's name when he was an angel," Jenna's voice deepened as she held steady eye contact with Sonih.

"I'll bring it to my colleague tomorrow morning. I'm sure it's some stupid prank," Will comforted the group with easy words.

2021.6.1

It was not unusual for Will to appear a few minutes prior to his first class or even a few minutes after on occasion, but this particular day curiosity brought him to the university hours before his first ten-o'-clock lecture. He waited outside Caleb Ethan's door. He was the history and religious science professor at the university and had become a good friend of Will's. Caleb had an easy spirit and a fiery sense of humor and brought a unique energy with his presence. He commonly greeted Will with great excitement, but on this particular morning, Caleb was concerned by the sight of his friend sitting on the ground outside his office cradling a stiffened piece of paper.

"Everything all right, bud?" Caleb offered.

Will looked up startled. He had been so engulfed in the delicate writing and mystery of the letter that he hadn't notice his friend's arrival.

"Not really," Will said matter-of-factly. "My kid got this in the mail." Will continued as he held the aged paper in the air for Caleb to examine.

"What is it?" Caleb inquired.

"I was hoping you could help me with that," Will informed hopefully.

"Sure, I'll try. I've got lecture in a few minutes. Do you want to sit in, and we'll review the document," Caleb suggested.

"I'd love to. My first lecture isn't until ten," Will accepted as Caleb fumbled through keys, trying to unlock his office door. Caleb stuffed a stack of papers from his desk messily into his briefcase and about-faced back toward the door. They walked down the hallway to the lecture room, where noisy students were already waiting.

Will found an open seat in the front row, pulled a tape recorder out of pocket, and rested it carefully on his lab.

"Students, as you see, Dr. Herrington is with us today. He brought an old document for us to interpret and determine authenticity," Caleb announced to the class. "It's signed 'Lucifer.' What do you think?" Caleb questioned.

A few students snickered, while a young man boasted aloud, "Isn't the devil supposed to be deceiving? Anyway, how can something not in this world write letters?"

One student reasoned aloud, "Obviously, it was written by a man, but the words were supposedly from Lucifer."

A nearby young woman rebutted while popping her gum. "Like a prophet, right, Professor Ethan?" she further inquired.

"I don't know, we'll see. First we'll have to interpret it, though. Get out your Latin translators," Caleb instructed while the students began fishing around in their bags for the requested book.

"Devin, could you read whom it's addressed to," Caleb coaxed.

"*Tennen De Lumen*," a boy spoke flatly.

"Anyone?" Caleb inquired while students flipped anxiously through their small dictionaries, writing the phrase on paper.

"Prince of hell," a young woman blurted nervously.

"Yes, now I want you to translate the whole letter," Caleb instructed while placing a handwritten form on the magnifier, sending a large image on the pull-down screen.

The students busily worked while Caleb returned papers to the students. After several moments, a young man raised his hand eagerly.

"Go ahead, Tanner," Caleb encouraged.

"Prince of hell, son of Lucifer, damned by birth. His blood will be empty. Child estranged from man. Man will call him Hellbound because his fate is set. Death will come by his own hand when Lucifer calls his name, then he will torment the damned beside his father rule for all eternity," The eager boy finished as nearby students looked at each other with surprise at the words.

"Good, Tanner. That's right," Caleb praised.

"Good. What's good about that?" Will yelled erratically while jumping to his feet.

Caleb looked over at Will with surprise. "It's just a letter, Will," Caleb tried to comfort.

Will stormed out of the lecture hall, tape recorder in hand, as Caleb quickly followed him into the hallway.

"What's going on, Will?" Caleb asked concerned.

"I call him Hellbound. It's just a stupid nickname because he was a pain-in-the-ass kid," Will spoke heatedly while pacing back and forth in front of Caleb.

"You know, I loved him, but he was difficult—resistant to everything I said. He was wild," Will explained.

"Will," Caleb spoke slowly and calmly, "this is just a letter. Most little boys are hyper. He sounds like a very strong, independent child."

"No," Will shouted. "I've treated children my entire career, Caleb. Jackson's not my real son. He was found on the street at about seven years old. He claimed he didn't have a family. He said he only remembered living on the streets, alone. Nobody would touch this kid. He was mean, vulgar, and out of control. The foster homes were overpacked, and he had potential to be violent. I took him in. It was supposed to be temporary, but I was scared to let him go. I don't know anyone who could have controlled this kid. I know I couldn't. Anyway, he had to do a paternity test for his son. He only had one strand of DNA, Caleb. The doctors said it was impossible," Will finished.

"It was probably just a fluke," Caleb insisted.

"They rechecked and rechecked, Caleb. They wanted to do all this thorough testing, but Hellbound refused," Will explained. "I mean, Jackson refused," Will corrected himself. "His son's blood has the same abnormality," Will continued nervously. "Leium isn't even Jackson's biological son. Sonih and Jackson, they say an angel came to each of them and told them Leium was God's son. That can't really be, right? I mean, I just reasoned it off to some fluke or unknown situation. What does that mean, Caleb?" Will rambled anxiously.

"Will, do you want to play hooky today? This is my only lecture today. I don't know any of the answers, but I may know how to find out," Caleb suggested.

"I'll call the dean and ask her to cover my class," Will agreed.

"All right, I'm going to go dismiss my class," Caleb informed Will.

Caleb grabbed a few books from his office before locking the door and meeting Will outside in the parking lot.

"Follow me," Caleb hollered while gliding in the seat of his Jeep Wrangler.

Will yelled, "OK," and proceeded to his Toyota Tercel. "I used to have a jeep," Will yelled meekly to Caleb, but Caleb who was already in the jeep with radio on failed to hear him.

Will jumped into his car and pulled up behind Caleb's jeep as it began to move. Twenty long minutes later, they arrived at Caleb's home. It was a new, ranch-style home, with gray siding and lots of windows. Will followed Caleb, who had books tucked under an arm, into the house. Caleb slid into a leather computer chair and rolled up to a large, wooded desk that was pushed up to a small window in the entranceway den.

"There should still be coffee in the kitchen. Do you want some?" Caleb offered while opening a laptop computer and turning it on.

"Sure," Will accepted as he wandered into the kitchen.

"Will you grab me a cup too, if there's enough?" Caleb hollered from the den.

"Yeah," Will responded while searching the cupboards for coffee mugs.

They sipped coffee while Caleb searched the internet, flipped through several books, and jotted notes onto a lined piece of paper.

"All right, I've got a good start," Caleb informed as Will listened eagerly. "There were ancient prophets long before Jesus's time, who predicted what was to come. I'm sure you're aware of that, but what less people are informed about are those that opposed God's will. The devil was once an angel of God named Lucifer, but he sought the power of God and betrayed God's will by trying to get other angels and people to worship him. God cast Lucifer and the other corrupt angels to hell," Caleb announced while Will shifted in his seat, still cradling the cup of coffee.

"Anyway, during these ancient times, Lucifer developed a small following of people on earth. He would speak to a select few and inform them of his plans to broaden his followers. This particular prophecy was written by his favorite prophet, Barrod. He writes a lot about a son that is to come and strengthen the devil's kingdom. Translations state that the devil will take a woman who is broken by addiction and use her to conceive a son. The son shall be left to harden alone in the streets. Food and clothes will be provided during the cover of night. It states his blood has been altered and marked as unique from man. He will rule the fires of hell beside Lucifer for all eternity, torturing lost souls and ascending to earth to help Lucifer's kingdom grow. When his time comes to rule, he will die by his own hand," Caleb explained.

"Suicide," Will clarified.

Caleb nodded, "Yes." And he continued to speak, "Jesus was also prophesied to make a second coming to earth, during this time the devil would use his son to attempt to corrupt God's son. It states his blood shall be marked unique as wel—that miracles shall surround his birth," Caleb finished.

"So the mother who promised her son to the devil, whatever became of her?" Will asked.

"It says it broke her mind and spirit, and she is forever haunted by Lucifer's following," Caleb responded.

"What am I supposed to do with this? Some crazy person obviously thinks this is Hellbound," Will blurted. "I mean, Jackson," Will corrected as Caleb shrugged his shoulders and raised his eyebrows with uncertainty.

"If it were me, I'd tell him the truth. Jackson's a strong man," Caleb offered.

Will nodded his head in acknowledgment.

"Well, I better go," Will said flatly. "I got a lot to sort through," Will added.

Caleb stood and shook his friend's hand.

"Just call or stop in if you need anything at all," Caleb emphasized.

PROPHECY

Will was waiting in Hellbound's kitchen, nursing a beer, when Hellbound and Sonih walked with Leium fast asleep in Hellbound's arms.

"How'd class go?" Will asked.

"Good," Sonih responded as Hellbound carried the sleeping child into his bedroom.

"Hellbound got a hundred percent on his anatomy test, and I studied twice as hard and only got an eighty percent," Sonih explained. "His memory is amazing," Sonih commented.

"It always has been," Will agreed as Hellbound reappeared from Leium's room and joined them in the kitchen.

"So what the pleasure?" Hellbound inquired of Will's late visit.

"Can't I just stop by?" Will asked.

"You can, but you don't," Hellbound stated before adding, "not this late, anyway."

"Do you want a beer?" Will offered, extending a long-neck bottle in Hellbound's direction.

"That bad, huh?" Hellbound anticipated.

Will raised his eyebrows and sat speechless, shifting his head slightly to the side.

"What'd he say?" Hellbound inquired sarcastically, while sitting down across the table from Will and accepting the beer from his hand.

"All right. I don't know how to say this any other way than to just come out and…" Will began rambling nervously.

"Just tell me," Hellbound demanded.

"OK, OK," Will submitted. "Some people may think you are the son of the devil, destined to rule beside him forever in hell," Will blurted out.

The kitchen was silent for moments before Hellbound erupted into laughter. Sonih furrowed her brow partly in distress by Will's comments and partly in confusion by Hellbound's reaction.

"And what do you believe?" Hellbound inquired.

"I don't know," Will responded. "A lot of weird stuff seemed to add up," Will added as Hellbound still snickered in the background.

Hellbound forced a hug on Will. "Listen, the letter startled me at first, but there are a lot of strange people out there. I'm in control of me, right? I'm not going to let one nutjob ruin even one of my nights," Hellbound reasoned. "And neither should you," Hellbound encouraged of his longtime friend.

They grew lost in tangles of conversation before Will reasoned he should let the young couple get some rest. Will parted after giving Sonih and Hellbound a last hug and reminding them how much he loved them.

Later that night, Sonih lay snuggled against Hellbound's shoulder, gentling pushing kisses on the side of his neck.

"I'm completely in love with you, Sonih," Hellbound whispered through the darkened bedroom.

"I know, sweets, and I'm completely in love with you, Hellbound," Sonih requited. "Forever," Sonih added.

"Forever," Hellbound agreed, both giggling like children.

"What do you think heaven is going to be like?" Sonih asked meekly.

"I guess like a glowing earth without any of the bad stuff," Hellbound suggested with a smile.

"Do you think there's any truth to what Will was talking about?" Sonih prodded skeptically.

"Yes," Hellbound blurted out, without offering any explanations.

"You think you're cursed?" Sonih challenged with surprise.

"Yeah, I do, Sonih. I feel as if there's a war sometimes going on inside me," Hellbound confessed. "Does that scare you?" Hellbound questioned.

"Hellbound, since the moment we met, I've felt as if there is something special about you—like, you're meant to do something wonderful. Yes, I guess, that terrifies me until I remember God is in charge," Sonih indulged as she shifted onto her elbow to try to find Hellbound's face in the darkness. "It scares me that I may not be strong enough. That someday, I may fail you," Sonih confessed. "But no, you don't scare me," Sonih added.

Hellbound smiled as a warmth flooded through him, and he kissed Sonih's warm lips.

"When are you going to give up on me, Sonih?" Hellbound asked smiling.

"Never. We're going to me together in Heaven for all eternity," Sonih promised.

Hellbound grabbed Sonih into a tight hug and planted a long, emotional kiss on her forehead, before they faded into sleep.

ABOUT THE AUTHOR

Courtney Sigler was born in Jackson, Michigan, October 21, 1980. She was blessed with three incredible sons—Austin, Randal, and Caleb—and an amazing husband, Mark. She enjoys her career as a nurse. For fun, she loves spending time outdoors with her family—canoeing, camping, or playing. Her hobbies include writing and cheering proudly for her sons at wrestling meets, baseball games, and whatever other activity they are participating in at the time. Look forward for new and bold twists from this passionate new author!

Cover art by Dione Tripp of Jackson, Michigan. Who is not only a boundless artist, but a dear friend. She tirelessly explores the multidimensional dynamics of colors, textures and movement, and embraces the use of both worldly and natural components to blend art and life in bold new ways. The power and passion she entwined in her breathtaking murals, evolved sculptures and captivating paintings is inspiring. Spirited by the Avant garde wea, she uses her ever examining depth to challenge truth through abstract and possibilities through invention.

CPSIA information can be obtained
at www.ICGtesting.com
Printed in the USA
FFHW020758110319
50964736-56380FF

9 781640 825314